PRAISE FOR DI

CW00521262

Just like the first in the series, it is a well-written, engaging, entertaining read. An excellent book, and one I could not put down!

— REVIEWER BELLE

Full of wry, witty observations on people and life that will have you reluctantly nodding in agreement or laughing out loud at their perceptive truthfulness, these books take you on a fun journey of self-discovery through the eyes of a teenage witch.

— AUTHOR HELEN PRYKE

What's a witch to do? I found myself rooting for Anais throughout the story. This is an interesting tale that will have you turning pages to find out what's next.

— REVIEWER KIMBERLEY

OTHER BOOKS IN THE SERIES

Visit **www.pjwhittlesea.com** for updates on releases.

DISCOVERING MAGIC

ANAÏS BLUE BOOK TWO

P J WHITTLESEA

Published by Tyet Books, Amsterdam

www.tyetbooks.com

information@tyetbooks.com

ISBN 9789492523211

Cover Design by Miblart

Edited by Philip Newey and Ella Holgate

For Zoé and every other child
who will remain forever young

Time present and time past
Are both perhaps present in time future,
And time future contained in time past.
If all time is eternally present
All time is unredeemable.

— EXCERPT FROM 'BURNT NORTON',
T. S. ELIOT 1888–1965

STARTING OVER

H i, it's me again.

Did you miss me?

If you're new to this tale you may want to go back and look at what happened earlier. For those of you who have no desire, or have forgotten, I won't penalise you for laziness. I will quickly refresh your memory and give you an overview. You do have a memory, don't you? Or are you a shade?

Let's start at the beginning. There is a witch. Yes, there are witches in this world. Real ones which keep the whole thing ticking along. Without them we would all be lost. The witch in question, our witch, is called Anaïs Blue, although she would prefer to be called something else. We won't concern ourselves with that. It is a problem she will have to deal with herself. Her purpose, and that of all witches, is to help the dead. Just as witches do, we shall call the dead *shades*. In these modern times we wouldn't want to insult anyone by using derogatory terms. The word shade is fairly neutral. At least, I think so anyway. I hope you agree.

The purpose of this book is personal. I need to tell you all I know before it's gone. My memory is fading—fast. I wish I could do something about this, but memories have a finite existence and mine is failing. I will not bother you with the details. I am of no great importance. The knowledge is.

Knowledge and information is the key to all this. Together we are trying to solve a very big problem. I am trusting you with something huge. It would be beneficial if we could keep all this information between ourselves. Let us consider it our little secret. Witches need freedom of movement. This is crucial. If everyone knew what I am about to tell you the entire system would cave in around our ears. Therefore—and I cannot stress the point too much—what I tell you is for your eyes only.

Consider yourself a confidant, a partner in crime if you will. However, we will try to avoid doing anything illegal. Be that real or supernatural. We don't want to cause anything untoward to happen. We have enough problems to solve as it is.

Where were we? Oh yes, one particular witch.

In previous exploits our witch, Anaïs, managed to survive a great many things: an enormous explosion, facing a witch high court, labouring with a deceased rock star and finding a solution to his predicament, a trip across the English Channel in a very small boat, inquisitors, hellhounds, family reunions, death and librarians. There is more in store for her, so read on.

I'll be back to keep you informed along the way, and remember, don't breathe a word to anyone. Guard this information carefully. You have a responsibility.

MORRIS THE MINOR

They had been cruising for some time before Immaculate Phlox spoke up. She had to yell to make herself heard above the car's cacophony. She flicked her head towards the rear of the vehicle. 'Who's your new friend?'

Anaïs cleared her throat. 'She's not new. She's an old friend.'

The shade's voice sounded in the little witch's head. *'I see you're still keeping nice company. Where did you pick her up?'*

Anaïs turned in her seat and faced the shade in the backseat. 'I didn't ask for her. She actually picked me up.'

'Oh will you stop doing that! It's rude,' said Immi. 'Can't you just think back at it instead of forcing me to listen to half a conversation?'

Anaïs swung around in her seat and sneered at the librarian. 'She can't read minds.'

She sat back in her seat and looked out her side

window at the trees whizzing by. 'Or at least I don't think she can.'

The little witch closed her eyes. *'Nan? Can you hear me?'*

'Always, child,' said Nan softly. *'It was the only thing that kept me going out there in the dark. I followed your voice and it brought me to you.'*

Anaïs smiled to herself. *'That's good to know. Nan, I missed you so much. I honestly thought I'd lost you. I'm so very sorry about what happened.'*

'You don't have to be sorry, Anaïs,' said Nan. *'You're safe now. That's all I care about.'*

'It's so good you're here,' replied Anaïs, sending out her thoughts. *'I thought I was alone. Well, maybe I'm not completely alone. I do have this waste of space to keep me company.'*

She opened her eyes and looked directly at the woman sitting next to her. 'What a douchebag!'

Immi looked hurt and pulled away from Anaïs. Furrowing her brow, she measured her response. 'What is wrong with the youth of today? No respect at all.'

Anaïs shot back at her. 'I'm sure you were young once, although I have my doubts.'

'Nice. Keep the insults coming. I'm all up for them,' said the librarian, sneering at the witch.

'Ok, ok, enough. Can the two of you stop bickering for a moment?'

The Morris Minor soared over a hump in the road and became airborne. Its passengers floated up off their seats and came crashing back down as the vehicle connected with the tarmac. Its springs bottomed out, producing a loud grating sound as all four wheels connected with the chassis. The Morris Minor switched off its radio. The impact and lack of music silenced its occupants.

The librarian and Anaïs looked at one another. Was the car aware of their altercations?

'How did you come into possession of this thing?' asked Anaïs, pointing at the dashboard.

The librarian struggled with making room for herself. Her oversized coat rode up on her, almost choking her. She grunted, tugged it down and settled back in her seat. She stared out the windscreen. 'It was waiting outside the airport when I arrived in England.'

'How did you know it was for you?'

'I was given an envelope containing a ticket and a set of keys. In the envelope was a note with instructions. It said a car would be waiting for me. Well, a car *was* waiting for me.'

The librarian scratched her head, using the tip of the slender, polished fingernail of her index finger in order to avoid messing up her hair. It was filed to a sharp point.

'Only, I expected a driver,' she said, looking down at Anaïs.

'How did you know which car?'

'It was kind of obvious. The car was parked at the entrance to the terminal and there was this,' said Immi. She reached across to the centre of the dashboard and lifted a cardboard tag which was attached to the car keys. She showed it to Anaïs. Written on the tag in immaculate calligraphy were two words: Morris Minor.

Anaïs smiled and nodded. 'Yeah, I guess that *is* kind of obvious. Were there any other instructions?'

'No.'

'Well, then, I don't get it. How did you find me?'

'I just got in the car and started driving. Whenever I had to make a turn it told me which way to go by switching on its indicators.' The librarian screwed up her nose. 'Honestly, I assumed the keys they gave me were magic and not the car itself.'

'Seems logical,' said Anaïs. She watched the key tag sway with the movement of the car. 'I just have one more question.'

The librarian sighed. 'What is it with small children and questions? You never seem to run out of them.' She looked down her nose at the little witch huddled in the seat beside her.

Anaïs folded her arms and huffed, 'I'm not a small child!'

'Fine,' said the librarian. 'One more question and then I'm going to have a nap.' She pulled her coat shut, hugged herself and went back to staring at the road. 'Chances are this could be a long ride and I'm kind of thankful I don't have to do the driving.'

Anaïs shuffled in her seat. 'Who gave you the envelope?'

'My mum, of course,' said the librarian matter-of-factly. 'Didn't you meet her in the library? Or at least someone who said she was her. Her name is Sojourner Pink.'

FAMILIES

Witches can't do it all alone. As previously mentioned, they need the help of normal, everyday human beings to get things done. There are thousands of wannabe witches out there, but they can only really be considered as a sort of fan club.

Fans of any kind are great, and who doesn't love a bit of adulation? However, not if they aspire to be something they're not—which is quite often the case once a fan becomes a confidante. People who desire something they cannot possibly have usually screw up the system.

Experience has taught witches that, in order to be left to do what it is they do best, they do not need competition getting in the way. Unless, of course, the competition makes a useful diversion. True assistance will only come from someone you can trust.

This is not to say that fans cannot be trusted. It is more that, once they have had a peek behind the scenes, they are usually in for a shock. More than likely, they are also in for a huge disappointment. Most people cannot cope with the reality hidden behind what props something extraordinary up. Generally, it is a lot more mundane and boring than expected. Maintaining a magical facade requires an inordinate amount of hard work. For most fans, this is no fun. They prefer to see results, and quickly. Otherwise, they will find something better to fill their time. They will move onto the next available icon to worship.

The day-to-day life of a witch is not particularly exciting. They are the same as you and me. They have to do their daily ablutions. Not to mention grocery shopping, cleaning, washing and other menial tasks. Then there is the decision about what to wear for the day.

Witches tend to have an extensive wardrobe, and deciding on the appropriate clothing for a day of witching can be quite tedious. This is especially the case when you are unsure of what you will be up against. All manner of supernatural and physical obstacles are likely to confront you. Choosing suitable attire is made all the more complicated when everything you own is stuffed into a hat. By the time you have rummaged through its contents, and laid it out on your bed—if you have one— you still have to decide what matches what. For this reason, witches tend to go for basic black. Although, in the case of Anaïs, purple was her preference. But then, Anaïs liked to be different.

These things, the basics, all have to be attended to before any work can be done. The average fan would get bored senseless waiting for anything magical to occur. Not that a witch's assistant is expected to do most of these things. They are primarily enlisted to smooth over the inadequacies of physical witch communication. And occasionally do their taxes.

One major requirement is that an assistant needs to be on call day and night. This is quite a stretch for an admirer, especially if the pay is not good. So, if a fan or supporter is of no use, then you need to find someone more reliable. Preferably someone close to home. An assistant who will not run off at a moment's notice and feels duty bound to the task they are given. Someone who is trained to be fully aware of their responsibilities. Someone who is mutually invested in the cause. Someone who feels morally obligated and who can be held accountable. Specifically, someone who is family.

Some find it a curse, others an honour, but, whenever possible, the task of being a witch's assistant usually falls to their offspring.

KERNAL PANIC

Anaïs snickered. 'Sojourner Pink is your mother!'

'Yes, of course. What's wrong with that?'

'Oh, nothing,' said Anaïs. 'Perhaps a little odd.'

'Odd?' squeaked the librarian. 'We all have to come from somewhere.'

'I know that. I'm sorry. I suppose I'm just a little surprised.'

'Probably not as surprised as she was when I popped out,' said the librarian with a smirk.

'Oh, so you were a mistake?'

The librarian's smile melted. 'I wouldn't know. I certainly hope not.' A troubled look clouded her face. 'I never thought to ask.'

Anaïs sensed she had insulted her. She reached across to pat her arm. The librarian retracted it. 'What are you doing?'

'I was trying to comfort you. I thought I'd said the wrong thing.'

'Why would you think that?'

'Oh, just because …' Anaïs was confused. 'Never mind.'

The librarian looked at her with consternation. 'Even for a witch, you're a little strange.'

Anaïs breathed out slowly. 'Maybe it's better if we don't discuss mothers?'

'Yes, maybe,' said Immi. 'Let's change the subject.' She nodded at the hat on the witch's head. 'Could you check your promptuary? I'd like to know where we're going.'

Anaïs brightened. 'Yes, good idea. So would I.'

She took off her beret and rummaged around inside.

'That's something I will never get used to,' said Immi.

'What?' Anaïs stopped what she was doing and looked at the librarian.

Immi pointed at the witch's arm which had disappeared up to the elbow into her beret. 'Your stump.'

'Oh this? Stump? Now who's the one with the strange sense of humour?'

'Peas in a pod,' said the librarian and grinned at her.

Anaïs found her promptuary and pulled it out. She placed it on her lap and set the beret back on her head. She opened the handbook.

'Map,' she commanded.

Nothing happened. The pages of the promptuary did not transform. They looked like the leaves of any ordinary book. Anaïs closed the handbook. She turned it over in her hands and scrutinised it. She opened it once more.

'Map,' she said forcefully.

Again there was no response. She slammed it shut and slapped the back cover. She opened the handbook and bent it back, cracking its spine. She flipped through its pages and stopped at the centre. She closed her eyes and concentrated. Clearing her mind, she focussed on the book.

'Map,' she pleaded softly.

She opened her eyes. The pages transformed momentarily, glowing bright blue.

Anaïs's eyes widened. There was an electrical crackle and then the glow dematerialised. Once again she was left staring at ordinary sheets of paper.

She was distraught. *What's going on?*

Anaïs held the book in front of her with both hands. She shook it. She yelled at it in frustration, 'Oh c'mon, work!'

There was no reaction from the promptuary. She closed the handbook and jammed her thumb down hard on the star in the centre of the front cover. It barely illuminated. It flickered sporadically on and off before emitting a slow, pulsing light. Anaïs set the book down on her knees and glared at it.

'I thought that thing could tell us where we're going,' said Immi.

'So did I,' said Anaïs. 'It wasn't the only thing it could do. Obviously there's something wrong with its supernatural circuitry, like it's locked in some form of sleep mode. It was working fine before.'

'When before?'

'In the town, before you-know-what happened.'

The librarian dipped her chin and looked over her sunglasses at Anaïs. 'Uh huh, so you think that had something to do with it?'

'How would I know? I just use the thing. I didn't make it. They didn't give me a manual with it. It *is* the manual.'

'Who is them?'

'The Organisation,' said Anaïs. 'They gave it to me a few years back. At least I think they did.' She pointed at the beret upon her head. 'They actually gave me this for a birthday. The promptuary was in it. I have no idea where it came from.'

Anaïs paused for a moment. 'Your mum's a member. Didn't she tell you anything about this sort of stuff?'

The librarian shook her head. 'No, she never tells me anything. Most of the time I wonder why I'm sworn to secrecy when nobody lets me in on any of their secrets.'

Anaïs picked up the promptuary and ran her finger around the contours of the star. 'There was a heap of energy running wild last night. Maybe it short circuited?'

'You mean like some kind of supernatural glitch has sent it haywire?'

Anaïs leaned back in her seat, rested her head on top of the backrest and stared at the roof of the Morris Minor. 'What do I know?'

The librarian sighed. 'Where does that leave us then?'

'We have the car,' said Anaïs.

'Yes, you have a point, but that's not exactly reassuring. At least, as far as I'm concerned.' She ran her eyes over the dashboard and stared at the needle quivering on the speedometer. 'It's fine if it knows where it's going, but I would kind of like to know as well.'

'I agree, but maybe we should just trust it?'

'Maybe, although I have to say there's not much I'm prepared to blindly trust any more.'

'Well, have you got any better ideas?'

'Nope,' said Immi. The two women stared at the road ahead.

The caretaker's voice rang in the witch's head. *'Why don't we all just relax, sit back and enjoy the ride.'*

The librarian swung around in her seat and looked down at the witch. 'Did you say something?'

'No, Nan did.' Anaïs furrowed her brow. 'Did you hear it?'

'I heard someone whispering,' said Immi.

'Wow, weird. Perhaps hanging around with a witch is starting to rub off on you.'

The librarian frowned. 'Don't say that. I could do without the complications.' She eyed the shade in the rear-vision mirror. 'What did she say anyway?'

'She told us to calm down,' said Anaïs.

'Calm down? I am calm.' She squirmed in her seat. 'I'd just like to know what's going on.'

'Wouldn't we all? Try being dead for a change and see how you like it,' said the caretaker dryly.

Anaïs hooted and burst into laughter.

'It's not funny,' said the librarian.

Anaïs covered her mouth and tried to stifle her giggling.

'Oh, yes it is,' she said, her voice muffled by her fingers. 'It's very funny.'

SUPERNATURAL SOFTWARE

Not everything in the witch world runs smoothly. Just as in our own world, there are glitches. Nothing is infallible. The forces of nature will conspire and cause stuff to fail or have minor hiccups. Nature has a way of shooting itself in the proverbial foot. There are no hard and fast rules to it. Nature is constantly in motion. The more you try to get your head around its workings, the more confusing it gets. Nature is an incredibly complex beast.

Witch's handbooks are rare objects. A witch does not choose a promptuary. There are no shops in which you can buy them. Purveyors of the occult will try to fob something similar off to you but you will be squandering your money. A promptuary cannot be bought. Nor can it be traded for that matter. If you are fortunate enough to receive one, it will be yours and yours alone. When the time comes, and presumably a promptuary knows when this is—they know everything else—a witch will receive their personal copy. Without one you cannot truly call yourself a witch. Once a promptuary has attached itself to your person it will never leave your side. Anaïs had already experienced this peculiar irritation. A book that just wouldn't leave her alone, would reveal itself at will and had a mind of its own. Unfortunately, now she had a book that wasn't worth the paper it was written on.

A small number of promptuaries have been discovered by naturals but, of course, no one has been able to get them to function. This is partly due to their not knowing what they held in their hands. To most naturals, it's just a book. To the human eye its contents are illegible. It is like having a toy or game in your hands and not being able to find the 'on' switch.

One example of a promptuary that has fallen into the wrong hands is the Voynich manuscript. For hundreds of years it has mystified naturals. Nobody knows exactly where it came from. There are stories of it originally being owned by a nobleman and then being handed on to someone else as a payment. In the days before international currency, trade in goods and service was more common. Long after the Romans came along and gave everybody loose change to jangle in their pockets, people continued trading in valuable objects. They still do it today.

There is much speculation as to who wrote the Voynich manuscript. On the surface it is constructed from a type of paper that was only available hundreds of years ago. The ink used on its pages is also not out of the ordinary for its pedigree. As far as old books go, it is just that—an old book. That is, until you open it.

The most curious things are written in it. The book contains an alphabet and illustrations. Yet no one has been able to understand them. Over the past century a number of the world's best cryptologists and decipherers have given it their best shot. Even the United States National Security Agency made attempts to decipher it in the 1950s. Not one expert has found the solution. Nobody has been able to crack the code.

At the very least they have concluded something very important. The contents of the Voynich manuscript are a code. On this point, they are correct.

The manuscript is one example of a promptuary that has had a supernatural software crash. It should have gone in for repairs. The book's binding appears to have been altered. It is missing its original jacket. Every promptuary has a star on its front cover, but not this one. This may go some way to explaining why it does not work. For those without the necessary knowledge, what it now contains is gobbledygook.

Its owner clearly did not have the ways or means to get it repaired and rather than seek a way to destroy it, which is also a difficult task, they misplaced it. Either that or perhaps the owner expired before they could do anything about it. Regrettably it fell into the hands of naturals. Fortunately, as long as it remains in its present state, it is harmless.

Witches are aware of its existence and it has served as a warning to those who are in possession of their own promptuary. Guard your handbook well. If something untoward should happen to your copy, you are responsible for its wellbeing. If it is in a defenceless state and cannot perform its usual magic, you must ensure it stays hidden, even if you cannot repair it.

In principle a natural should not be able to decipher a promptuary, but there are no guarantees. What naturals lack in knowledgeable management of the universe they make up for with ingenuity. One danger is that a handbook, in such a state of disarray, could attach itself to the wrong person. Someone without the knowledge to use it properly. Even worse, the code could be cracked. In the case of the Voynich manuscript there is the risk that maybe some hacker will stumble upon a way to reboot it. Then they could conceivably manipulate its power to wreak havoc. One step further, and a worst case scenario, is if naturals found a way to reproduce its inner workings. Then we would all truly be in trouble. Virtually anyone could get access to a copy.

Thankfully none of this has happened, but we do not want to go tempting fate. Uncontrollable power in the hands of novices is never a good thing.

AN APOLOGY

Anaïs wriggled in her seat. It was getting uncomfortable. She also sensed the need for a toilet break. She turned to the librarian. 'Do you think we can make this thing stop? I think I need to take a leak.'

Immi sat with her arms folded across her chest, her eyes shooting over the hedgerows as they flew by.

'Do I look like I'm the one in control here?' She nodded at the steering wheel in front of her. It twitched left and right, keeping the vehicle centred on the bitumen. She snarled. 'You're the witch. Why don't you ask it?'

'I never thought of that,' said Anaïs. She scratched her head. 'I'll give it a try.' She reached out and stroked the smooth metal dashboard. 'Please stop,' she said softly.

Immediately, the Morris Minor cut its engine and slowed. Immi raised an eyebrow, pursed her lips and looked down at Anaïs. 'Next time, I'll just let you drive.'

Anaïs grinned. 'Cool!'

'I was joking,' said Immi. 'It's far from cool. I don't think letting you drive is a good idea. You can't even see over the steering wheel. I certainly hope this thing doesn't listen to you too much.'

The smirk spread wider across Anaïs's face. Immi put her head in her hands and shook it. The car pulled over to the side of the road and stopped in a gap between the hedgerows.

'I'll be right back,' said Anaïs.

'I doubt I'll be going anywhere without you,' sniped the librarian.

Anaïs batted her eyelids at her. She unlatched her door and pushed it open with both legs. She stepped out of the vehicle and slammed the door behind her. Beyond the hedgerow was an open field. She walked out into it, the frost-coated grass crunching under her shoes. She took in the view. The need to relieve herself faded. It hadn't been what had driven her out of the car. She really just wanted a moment to herself. She breathed deeply.

Anaïs adjusted the sunglasses on her nose. She lifted them up and peeked out under them. She decided the purple tint suited her better than the natural light and dropped them back on her nose. She adjusted them so that they hooked more securely over her ears. She thought about the shade she had just saved and smiled to herself, once again thanking him silently for his gift.

'Nice view.'

Anaïs jumped in surprise. She whirled around. Nan was so close the witch's face became buried in the folds of the shade's overcoat. She sucked in her breath and recoiled in shock. Stepping away from her caretaker, she turned, exhaled and waited until her thumping heart settled. 'Can you not sneak up on me like that?'

'Sorry for startling you, I'm still getting used to this myself.'

'That doesn't surprise me.' Anaïs pulled her beret down low over her ears and looked out at the undulating fields before her. She shivered, feeling the chill of the shade hanging on her shoulder. It was cold even without the addition of its aura. 'And yes, you're right, it is a nice view.'

Anaïs closed her eyes. She sniffed and rubbed her nose. 'I'm sorry,' she said.

There was no response from Nan. Anaïs sensed she was not ready to accept apologies. She pondered their situation and realised facing your killer, even if the act was unintentional, could not be an easy thing to do. She decided to try another approach. Perhaps it would help if they discussed the events which led them to their present predicament.

'What happened, Nan?'

'What do you mean?'

'To you,' said Anaïs. 'What happened to you?'

Nan considered her question for a moment. *'You mean before all this, in Amsterdam?'*

Anaïs nodded.

'I don't remember much, only darkness. Lots and lots of darkness.'

'And before the darkness, before *it* happened, do you remember anything?'

'I was in the kitchen and the doorbell rang.'

'That's it?'

'Yes.'

'And after that?'

'Nothing else. Like I said, darkness. I was in the kitchen making you lunch and it was as if a curtain dropped. Then it lifted. Suddenly, there I was, standing on a street in Cornwall with you. We are in Cornwall, aren't we? I saw some signs.'

Anaïs looked over the field at the horizon. Running along it she could see the blue line of the ocean. 'Yes, we are in Cornwall, although I have no idea where exactly.'

'So we are both lost.'

'Yes,' said Anaïs.

'No matter, at least we are together. Like I was saying, I was standing there on the street. Except I wasn't myself any more. Something was missing.'

'Life?'

'Well, yes, life. But somehow I still feel alive. Numb, but alive.'

'Shall I tell you what really happened?' asked Anaïs.

'I'm not sure I want to know. I worked out the obvious. I know I died.'

Anaïs heard Nan take a deep breath. It was the strangest thing and something she could not adjust to— the sound of a dead person breathing in her head.

'Somehow that doesn't seem to bother me. Death is clearly not the end. I'm here now, right?'

Anaïs nodded. She wasn't sure if she should feel sad or happy that Nan was still around. She felt incredibly guilty about the whole thing and could not bring herself to look at the shade. She looked down at the wet grass at her feet and concentrated on the voice in her head.

'Although, I'm sure I look different. You know, with the camouflage and all that.'

'Yes, you do look different. Maybe we can find you a mirror so you can look at the real you. That worked before.'

Reluctantly, Anaïs turned to face her caretaker. It took her breath away. Nan looked exactly as she had on that last fateful day in Amsterdam. It was astounding. The shade she had come face to face with, back on the street in Lizard, had looked very different. It only had Nan's voice. She now saw the real Nan, her Nan—the living, breathing Nan. Not the crushed, lifeless corpse in the ruins of their apartment building, but the woman she had last seen standing in the doorway of the dining room in Amsterdam. Before the strange woman had swept her into her arms. Before the building had collapsed into a pile of rubble.

Anaïs played the scene back through her mind. She wondered where she was now. The woman who was still a mystery. The one who had caused all of this. Was she watching them? Was she following them? And, not only that, what of the man and his dog? What had happened to them? Were they all gone forever? Were there others out there searching for her? She sensed she wasn't safe. If it was possible for Nan to find her, the chances were, anyone could.

The caretaker snapped her out of her thoughts. *'Well, do I look different?'*

'What?' Anaïs stopped staring into space and looked at Nan again. 'Sorry, what did you say?'

'Do I look different?'

Anaïs shook her head. 'No. It's amazing. You don't look any different to how you did before. I don't get it.' Anaïs scratched the back of her head and adjusted her sunglasses.

'*And without them?*'

'Without what?'

The nanny pointed at Anaïs's face. '*What do I look like without the sunglasses?*'

Anaïs took off the glasses. Everything lost its soft, purple hue. The nanny changed. Her camouflage materialised. Anaïs assessed the shade. 'Wow! It is the glasses!'

'*So, how do I look without them?*'

'You look like an older, fatter you,' said Anaïs.

'*Great! All that work to keep my figure in shape and then death hands me obesity.*'

'Nan! No, it's not that bad. I think you look pretty good for your age.'

'*Anaïs, don't feed me crap. You know I can see through you.*'

'But—'

'*No buts! If I could see more than just the tips of my shoes, I might believe you.*'

Anaïs shuffled her own feet nervously.

'*Tell me the truth! Now!*'

Anaïs stepped away from Nan. She spoke so softly she could barely be heard. 'You look like your mother.'

'*Oh god, no! No way! That's too much! Anyone but her!*' She stamped her foot so hard Anaïs felt the ground tremble. '*That's it. I don't want to be dead any more!*'

'If there was anything I could do about it, I would,'

said Anaïs sheepishly. 'I feel guilty enough about the whole thing as it is.'

'Good,' snapped Nan. *'I hope you're suffering.'*

Anaïs glowed red, avoided Nan's glaring eyes, and began fiddling with the buttons on her jacket. 'I am.'

'How do you know what my mother looks like anyway?'

'You showed me a picture once.'

'Oh, did I? I thought I destroyed them all.'

'You did. I saw the last one before you threw it on the fire.'

'Oh.'

Anaïs bit her lower lip. 'I met your mother when you were gone.'

'Really?'

'Yes, she was quite upset.'

'Surprising. I can't imagine that. I thought she had a heart of stone.'

'I got that impression myself. Now you say it, I'm not sure if it was grief or anger.'

'Probably the latter. I can't believe she really misses me.' There was a sharp edge to her voice. *'Can we change the subject? The less I hear about her the better.'*

The little witch nodded and stared glumly at the ground between the caretaker's feet. Nan simmered in silence.

Anaïs started to blubber. 'I wish I could change all this. I wish … I want you back, Nan. I want the real you. I-I'm so sorry.' Her lips trembled and then she lost it. Tears streamed down her face.

Nan expanded her chest and took a moment to compose herself. She moved towards the little witch and slid an arm around her shoulders. She pulled Anaïs's head to her breast. The sudden chill caused Anaïs to shiver involuntarily.

The caretaker spoke softly, almost in a whisper. *'I know you are, Anaïs. I forgive you. None of us could have known what would happen. The last thing I want is for you to have to carry around feelings of guilt about it. What's done is done. The main thing is I am still here, no matter what form that is. Together, we will work this out.'*

Anaïs sniffed, ran her arm under her nose and wiped a line of snot along her sleeve. She looked for somewhere to wipe the sleeve. Finding nothing she rubbed it down the front of her jacket.

Nan released her grip and stepped back. She pulled a face at Anaïs. *'I see we still have a lot of work to do on your manners. And that's something that could take eons.'*

Anaïs smiled and chuckled through her tears. She snorted more snot down her front. She used the other sleeve to clean her face.

Nan shook her head in dismay. *'I have a sneaking suspicion that's why I'm still around. Clearly, the powers that be won't allow me to leave until you've learnt the meaning of the word etiquette.'*

Anaïs grinned at her. 'I hope you're up to the job.'

Nan looked sternly at her. *'It'll be tough, but I'm no quitter, Anaïs.'*

The little witch nodded. 'I know, although I'm not sure if hanging around me is a curse or a blessing.'

Nan smiled. *'Believe me, it's a curse. But I was never one to take the easy route.'*

'That makes two of us.'

The nanny raised her hand. *'Partners in chaos?'*

Anaïs slapped it. 'Partners in chaos!'

Nan straightened. *'Enough of this soppy crap. Let's go do something constructive.'*

Anaïs beamed her broadest smile and nodded enthusiastically. 'Yes, let's!'

MARAZION

The Morris Minor careened around a blind corner, the trees and hedgerows disappeared and all of a sudden everything opened up before them. They drove along the crest of a hill. Down below them the road snaked its way along the face of the hill and entered a small fishing village where it terminated at a port. Out in the sheltered bay was an island. It was dominated by an impressive fortress. The structure was perched on the pinnacle of the only hill on the island. Tiers of high stone parapets encircled a central tower block. There was very little land visible on the island save for the odd small patch of grass. The stony outcrops of the fortress seemed to sprout out of the earth and it appeared as if the entire structure had risen out of the sea.

The Morris Minor swung around a tight curve and plunged down the hillside. Within moments they entered the narrow streets of the village, obscuring Anaïs's view of the bay. The road tapered into a single lane. The solid stone houses flanking it were uncomfortably close as they flashed by. Without reducing its speed, the car mounted the footpath to avoid a parked vehicle. Its engine maintained a constant whine which was barely audible, drowned out by the radio that had resumed blasting out the Queen song in constant repetition.

As they passed precariously close to yet another parked car, Anaïs gritted her teeth and shot a look across to the librarian. Sitting next to her, Immaculate Phlox seemed unperturbed and actually appeared to be enjoying the ride. She sat deep in her seat with her arms folded across her chest, her eyes flitting over houses as they shot by her only movement. Anaïs sensed she knew more than she was giving out. The breakneck speed of the ride and loud noise gave her no opportunity to ask questions.

She closed her eyes, her heart beating fast. Nan's soothing voice rang in her head. *'It's ok, Anaïs, the car will keep us safe.'*

Anaïs thought Nan was reassuring herself as much as she was trying to calm her. Nevertheless, the caretaker's voice gave her some comfort.

The little car slewed around a long, sweeping curve, then snapped suddenly in the opposite direction. Its wheels screeched in earnest on the cobblestones as it dove down a side street. Anaïs tightened her grip on the edge of her seat as she was thrown sideways. She heard the metallic clang of the car's rear fender, clipping the corner of the house bordering the intersection. An even smaller street confronted them. Mercifully it was short. The car threaded through a gateway at the end of the street and out into an empty parking lot. They flew across the open space and headed straight towards an impenetrable-looking stone wall. The Morris Minor engaged its handbrake. The back end of the vehicle swung out, sending them into a clockwise spin of almost 270 degrees. The car ground momentarily to a halt.

Before them lay a boat ramp leading down to a wide stretch of beach.

The little car gunned its engine, launched itself forward, pinning everyone to their seats, and roared down the ramp and out onto the beach. The Morris Minor lurched over the irregular sandy undulations, throwing its passengers around in their seats. It flew over a particularly large mound of sand, lifting them off their seats as it had done earlier, and jolting them back down. This time it took the wind out of Anaïs. A small, flat-topped ferry stood at the water's edge. The car cut its engine and silenced the radio. It locked its brakes as it neared the waterline. It slid the last few metres across hard, wet sand and mounted a ramp protruding from the ferry. It ended its journey, gliding to a smooth halt and making gentle contact with the guardrail at the bow of the boat. It rolled backwards. The handbrake between the front seats popped up and the car stopped.

The occupants of the vehicle released their breath in unison. Anaïs even heard the sound of Nan's exhale whistle past the inside of her ears. Across the calm waters of the bay, and only a short distance away, the vista of the island fortress loomed before them.

SAINT MICHAEL'S MOUNT

'**S**hall we do that again?' enquired the librarian with a sarcastic grin.

'I'd rather not,' said Anaïs, looking warily at the Morris Minor. 'I prefer to know where I'm going.'

Anaïs and Immi had got out of the car and stood in front of it at the bow of the ferry. The boat pootled quietly across the bay, its motor barely audible over the sound of water sloshing against the hull. The sea was dead calm, the morning sun reflecting off its glassy surface. There was a refreshing bite to the cold air. Anaïs pulled the collar of her jacket snug around her neck and watched the town of Marazion shrink behind them. She turned her attention to their destination.

The island fortress of St Michael's Mount was silent and ominous. A small group of seagulls circled around its turrets. Apart from the birds the island appeared lifeless. Anaïs looked around the ferry. There was neither a boathouse nor a pilot. She could feel the vibrations of a motor beneath her feet. They were being guided by an invisible navigator but physical forces certainly powered the flat-topped boat.

The ferry glided across the water and entered a small fortified harbour. It was ringed by a high stone wall that rose out of the ocean. A few small fishing boats were moored to the wall. Otherwise the whole place was deserted. The ferry cut across the middle of the harbour and aimed directly for a boat shed. The doors of the shed opened and the ferry entered. As the shed's doors closed behind them they were plunged into darkness.

There was a whine as somewhere at the rear of the shed antiquated machinery cranked into action. This was followed by the throb of a pump and the sound of water being sucked into a tube. Anaïs felt the floor beneath her feet shudder. The ferry was no longer floating but seemed to have sunk onto something solid. There was a final gurgle of water and the sound of suction ceased. This was followed by the whir of flywheels spinning up and the sound of enormous cogs squeaking and grinding. A ratchet clanked. She heard loud ticking as its pawls ran over its teeth. It found purchase and engaged its gearing. Everything creaked and groaned.

The ferry lurched violently forward and Anaïs was thrown onto the bonnet of the Morris Minor behind her. She ran her hand over the curve of the bonnet and searched in the dark for something to secure herself with. Finding the warm grill of the car nestled at the base of her spine, she turned and slid her fingers between the slits. She grabbed hold of it with both hands. Only then did she cry out.

'Immi?'

'I'm here.' The librarian's wavering voice sounded in the dark a few metres away.

'Good—I think.' Anaïs peered into the darkness but could see absolutely nothing. 'Nan? What's going on?'

'I'm here, Anaïs. I don't know. Your guess is as good as mine.'

Anaïs closed her eyes and focussed on the noises. The floor beneath her rocked from side to side and then began moving. They were descending, fast. Her feet didn't leave the floor but she felt a reduction in the effect of gravity. Were they free-falling? Her stomach sank and then adjusted itself. The downward journey continued for several minutes. The dank smell of mould rose under Anaïs's nostrils and the air became considerably cooler. Their descent slowed. There was a rumble and grinding of gears, and then a solid clunk as they came to a halt.

The Morris Minor started its engine, purring into action. Anaïs instinctively withdrew her hands from the grill and spun around. In front of her, a heavy steel door crashed to the floor. It left a ringing in her ears. The librarian yelled out in panic.

She cried out herself. 'Immi? Nan?' There was no response from either of the women.

The Morris Minor inched forward, nudging Anaïs with it. Steadying herself, with her hands behind her on its bonnet, she let the little car push her. With each step she patted her foot gingerly on the floor in front of her and tried to feel for something stable. The car stopped. To her right Anaïs heard the sound of a lock unlatching. A wall slid to one side and bright light flooded in.

Anaïs squinted and blinked several times. Adjusting

her eyes to the light, she took in her surroundings. They were in what seemed to be a small garage. The walls and ceiling were constructed entirely of dark timber panelling. The wall to her right was not a wall at all, but an enormous wooden door. Outside, a narrow cobbled pathway ran past the opening. Facing her and a few metres away, a solid stone wall bordered the other side of the path. Immaculate Phlox stood with her back to the timber wall of the shed in front of Anaïs. Her arms were splayed out at her sides with her palms flat against the woodwork. Her breast heaved.

She noticed Anaïs looking at her. The panic on her face dissolved and she regained her composure. She eyed Anaïs with her usual unamused demeanour. She muttered under her breath, 'Next time, remind me to stay in the car.'

Before Anaïs could respond there were footsteps on the path outside. Both women turned to face the opening. The fingers of a pristine white glove appeared and wrapped themselves around the door frame. They were followed by the pale, round face of a rather jovial looking old man. His cheeks glowed red and an enormous moustache ran under his nose, covering half his face. His whiskers were skilfully twirled to a point at each end. His skull was decked with an ushanka. Its sheepskin flaps covered his ears and framed his face.

He flashed them a toothless grin, opened his mouth to speak and then reconsidered. Stepping fully into the doorway he fumbled in the side pocket of his greatcoat. He made a fist and tugged at its contents. With a grunt he pulled out his hand. Opening his palm, he revealed a set of dentures. He shoved them into his mouth, snapped his jaw shut and then clicked his teeth together a few times. He cleared his throat.

'My apologies,' he said. 'I was forgettin' me manners.'

He pulled the glove off his right hand and proffered it to Anaïs. 'Welcome, Miss Blue. Let me help you down. We've been expecting you. Did you have a nice trip?'

THE LOCOMOTIVE

The locomotive wheezed loudly as if it were suffering from a debilitating lung condition. It was gigantic and practically filled the tunnel. Standing beside it, Anaïs craned her neck, tilting her head back and taking in its enormity. Its silver-coated bulk gleamed as if it had just come off the factory floor and never been in use. Anaïs smiled and her face lit up. It was quite something to behold.

After they had left the wooden shed, which in reality was a carriage at the rear of a train, the old man had proclaimed himself the engineer of the vehicle. He had led the way down the platform. Anaïs had followed him to the driver's cabin. He had climbed a ladder on the side of the locomotive and stepped inside. He now stood in the doorway, leaning against the frame.

He reached into his greatcoat and, from a tartan waistcoat, pulled out a silver fob watch. He checked the time. Not unlike the locomotive, the watch was an instrument of generous proportions. He balanced it in the palm of his hand, the tips of his fingers barely wrapping around its edges. It trailed a heavy silver chain. The links disappeared into the folds of his greatcoat.

The engineer flipped the watch over in his hand. Vapour hissed out through a tiny hole on its circumference. It appeared to be steam powered. He removed the glove from his free hand and pried open a small lid on its rear face. Bending down, he ran his fingers along the floor at his feet. Coal dust coated the tips of his fingers. He ground it between his fingertips and funnelled it into the hole. There was a flare and a lick of flame shot out. The engineer pulled his head back quickly, to avoid singeing his eyebrows. He snapped the little lid shut, turned the watch over in his hand and once again consulted the dials on its face. He pulled on his white glove and polished the instrument. From his perch he looked down his nose at the little witch and sighed.

'There was a time when I had a little more assistance,' he declared. 'I would ask you to help but once this thing is up and running it's better not to be up here.' The engineer checked his watch again. 'We have a few minutes. Would you like to take a look?'

Anaïs grinned up at him. 'Would I ever?'

The engineer knelt on one knee, gripped the door frame of the cabin and reach down. He flipped his fingers at her. Anaïs grabbed his hand.

He bared his dentures and winked at her. 'All aboard!' he cried.

For such an old man he was surprisingly strong. In

one fluid, effortless motion he pulled her up, standing as he did. She gripped her arm with her other one to prevent it being wrenched out of its socket. She felt like a fish hanging from a line. The engineer took a step back, spun a half turn and deposited her in the cabin beside him.

Even in the relatively dim light of the cabin the engine sparkled and glinted. Anaïs had half expected to see a soot-covered lump of ancient machinery. This was something altogether different. There were all the usual makings of a steam engine: a coal furnace throwing off heat from its fire chamber, and all manner of cranks, cogs, levers and dials. Except, instead of being black, the machinery and mechanisms were silver plated and spotless. Anaïs could practically see her own reflection in the apparatus.

She turned her attention to the engineer. 'It's marvellous!'

The engineer took in the incredulous look on her face. He blushed. 'Thank you. You're too kind. I've had a lot of time on my hands. Unfortunately we don't get many passengers nowadays.' He puffed himself up with pride. 'However, as you can see, it has given me plenty of opportunity to keep the beast finely tuned.' He lovingly caressed one of the dials and buffed it to a shine with the soft edge of his gloved hand. 'She's quite something, isn't she?'

Anaïs nodded enthusiastically. She reached out and touched one of the knobs closest to her. The engineer shooed her away and rubbed the fingerprint away with a gloved thumb.

He shook a white finger at her. 'No fingerprints please.' He put his hands on his hips and looked around the cabin.

'You may touch this, though,' he said, indicating a thick rope slung above her head. 'Here, let me help you.'

The engineer knelt down and picked her up. He balanced her on his shoulder.

'Go ahead, pull it,' he said.

He was clearly fixated with keeping his machine immaculate and Anaïs was wary of touching anything.

The engineer sensed her trepidation. 'It's ok,' he said. 'Go ahead, pull it.'

She reached up and grabbed the rope. She had to pull with both hands as there seemed to be quite a bit of weight behind whatever it was connected to. As soon as she had done so, she regretted it.

A great, thunderous horn bellowed out just above her head. The noise made her duck. Anaïs clapped her hands around her ears and grimaced. It sounded more like the foghorn of an ocean liner than a train and had approximately the same volume. The noise was made even louder by the confined space in the tunnel. The reverberations continued to echo off the solid stone walls for some time. Eventually they were swallowed up by the brickwork.

Anaïs jiggled a little finger in her ear and flexed her jaw. The engineer chuckled at her and turned his head to one side. He pulled up one of the flaps on his hat and showed her a wad of cottonwool jammed into his ear.

He winked and smiled at her. 'Sorry, I should have warned you.'

When he smiled she noted the blackened build-up of coal dust between his dentures. He bent over and set her down. Pulling the instrument out of his coat, he consulted his watch once again.

'Time to go,' he said. 'I could use the companionship but you better get down now. Unfortunately we have rules.'

'Pity,' she said.

'There's nothing to see really. You'll be safer in the carriage.'

'Safer?'

'You'll see,' he said.

Anaïs climbed down the steps of the ladder and dropped herself onto the platform. She hesitated and looked up at him.

He cocked his head towards the rear of the train. 'Go on now. I'll see you at the other end.' He stepped back and gently closed the cabin door with a click.

Anaïs looked around her. The platform was deserted. Above her, the vaulted tunnel arched over her head. The brickwork was intricate, each individual stone hand painted. She was pleased to see a proliferation of purple. Dwarfed by the enormity of the locomotive, she stepped back to admire it once more. It was an impressive piece of machinery. Emblazoned on its side in bold lettering were the words: PUFFING DEVIL.

A blast of steam shot out from its underbelly. She jumped back to avoid it but the cloud caught her in a warm hug. It completely enveloped her and obscured everything. She waved her hands in front of her face to clear it but with little effect.

A clear, loud, male voice sounded in the mist. 'Miss Blue?'

'Thistle,' Anaïs murmured to herself.

Again the voice called out in the fog. 'Miss Blue, this way please.'

Anaïs followed the sound of the voice, feeling her way out of the cloud of steam and walking towards it down the platform. As the steam cleared, it revealed a man smartly dressed in a nineteenth-century uniform. The breast of his coat was decorated with two lines of shiny buttons. Wide, stiff epaulets sat on his shoulders like two thin planks of wood. A box-shaped cap adorned his head, with the small peak pulled down low over his eyes. He stood on the platform in front of the door to the train's solitary passenger carriage. It was coupled behind the coal tender.

As she approached him, he opened the door with one hand and stepped back. He waved with his other hand, indicating that she should board. Anaïs stopped in front of him and studied his face. It was the engineer. Or at least she thought it was. The two men's faces were identical. The only difference, this man's face lacked the engineer's handlebar moustache. This version of him was clean shaven. She furrowed her brow. It seemed pretty unlikely he had managed to shave in the short time it had taken to get from locomotive to carriage.

'But—' stammered Anaïs.

The man gave her a friendly smile. 'Is there a problem, madam?'

She pointed at the locomotive. 'Weren't you just in—'

He shook his head. 'No, that would be my brother. He's the engineer and I'm the conductor.'

She scratched her head. 'I see. But he said he was alone.'

'Please stop dillydallying, Miss Blue,' said the conductor, impatiently. 'We have a schedule to keep.'

Anaïs folded her arms, stood her ground and glared up at him. 'My name is Miss Thistle!'

The conductor took a deep breath. He straightened his overcoat by pulling on the front panel and smoothing it down. He systematically checked the buttons on his jacket. He tilted his head from side to side and stretched, cracking the bones in his neck. Finally, he straightened his arms and yanked down on his sleeves, snapping them taut. He fixed Anaïs with a stern look. 'As you wish. Now please board the train, Miss Thistle.'

There was another tremendous blast from the horn of the locomotive. A fresh jet of steam shot from its underbelly and rolled down the platform towards them. Anaïs leapt in surprise at the sound and scooted up the steps.

The conductor blew his whistle, mounted the steps and swung the door shut behind him. Anaïs stood in the vestibule watching him. The train jolted forward, almost throwing them off their feet. It then settled into a slow trundle.

The conductor unlatched another door, leading into the carriage itself. He set a hand on the little witch's shoulder and gently guided her through the doorway. 'Please hurry and take a seat, Miss Thistle.'

Anaïs stepped through the doorway and surveyed the interior of the carriage. Her jaw dropped.

'Wow!' she exclaimed.

THE DINING CAR

Anaïs stood in awe, staring at the ceiling. It was arched and constructed entirely of glass. Where it joined the wall, an intricately carved cornice ran around the circumference of the room. What she saw through the glass mesmerised her. The ceiling was, in fact, some form of enormous skylight.

Above her, Anaïs could see dark clouds swirling. A storm was brewing. Occasionally a wayward leaf floated by. Seagulls hovered on thermal draughts and swept in and out of view. Droplets of rain hit the glass intermittently and ran in rivulets down the sides of the domed structure. In the corner of the skylight, Anaïs could see one of the turrets from the island fortress. It gradually disappeared from view. They were moving away from the island and out to sea. The seagulls were left behind and the sky began to clear. The storm clouds that had been building receded into the distance and gave way to pristine blue sky.

None of it computed and Anaïs wondered how it

was possible to see all of these things. They were perhaps hundreds of metres under the sea. There was no indication the glass was a video screen. What she saw was not a projection. She was looking through a window.

The sun revealed itself and illuminated the entire room. It glinted off a crystal chandelier, which hung in the middle of nowhere. It was suspended from a ceiling rose that seemed to float in the sky. Strangely, there was still the feeling they were on a train. Anaïs felt the vibrations beneath her feet and the soft sideways sway of the carriage. Even the chandelier shuddered.

The ceiling was not the most impressive thing about the carriage. The interior of the carriage was completely out of proportion with its exterior. It was huge. She stood in an expansive hallway which had the dimensions of a sprawling eighteenth-century mansion and looked like one too. Floating staircases ran up both side walls and joined together at a small landing one storey above. Under the landing was a set of double doors. They were open and led through to a rather grand-looking dining room.

Through the doors Anaïs could see Nan and Immi seated at a long, heavy oak table that split the dining room. The table laboured under a vast amount of food. The librarian was stuffing handfuls of it into her mouth and wolfing it down. Nan sat opposite her with a look of dismay clouding her eyes.

Anaïs took a step back to admire the room she was in. She bumped into the man standing behind her.

'Oops, sorry,' she said apologetically.

The man carefully measured his words and spoke with an impeccable Oxford English accent. It was not the voice of the conductor. 'No need to apologise, madam.'

Anaïs spun to face him. He was identical to the engineer and the conductor, save for a set of generous mutton-chops. He was dressed in a stiff butler's uniform: a black suit with swallow-tails, grey waistcoat, starched white shirt with winged butterfly collar and a thin black tie. His leather shoes were buffed to a high shine.

'You've got to be kidding,' Anaïs muttered under her breath.

'Excuse me, madam?'

'Er, you wouldn't be related to the conductor by any chance?'

'Why yes, madam, he is my brother,' replied the butler.

'And the engineer? Is he your brother as well?'

'Certainly, madam.'

Anaïs cocked her head. 'There wouldn't, by any chance, be any more of your brothers floating around here somewhere?'

The butler slowly shook his head. 'No, madam, not that I'm aware of.'

'Good.'

'Is there anything else you would like to know, madam?'

'I don't think so,' said Anaïs.

'Excellent! May I take your coat, madam?'

Anaïs hesitated.

The butler smiled at her. 'It's ok, madam, I will give it back.'

Anaïs smiled back at him and nodded. She slipped off her coat and handed it to him. He folded it and slung the coat over his arm. He held out his free hand. 'And your hat, madam?'

Anaïs reached up and placed her hand on her beret. 'No, I'd prefer to keep it on. And can you please stop calling me madam.'

'As you wish.' He stepped to one side. 'Would you care to follow me, miss? Breakfast is served.'

Anaïs frowned. 'Breakfast?'

'Yes, or have you already eaten?'

'No, I just forgot the time of day.'

'Of course,' said the butler. 'I fully understand. The tunnel does tend to confuse the senses.'

Anaïs looked up at the skylight. The sun went momentarily behind a cloud and a shadow flitted across the room.

The butler indicated the dining room. 'Shall we?'

Anaïs nodded and followed him across the hall and into the room. The butler wrapped her jacket around a coathanger and hung it in a rack next to the door. He walked over to the table and pulled out a chair. He offered her the seat. She climbed up on it and let him slide the chair back under the table. For Anaïs the tabletop was neck high, her chin resting on its edge.

She looked up at the butler. 'Do you have a cushion for me?'

The butler saw her predicament. His eyes widened. 'My apologies, miss. One moment please. A cushion will not be necessary.' He flipped a switch on the rear of the chair and it began to rise. Once Anaïs was waist high with the table, he flipped the switch a second time and the chair stopped moving.

'Is this better, miss?'

'Perfect!' Anaïs grinned at him. 'Thank you very much.'

The butler stepped away from the table and clasped his hands behind his back. 'A pleasure to be of service, miss. If there is nothing more, I have matters to attend to.'

Anaïs nodded. 'I think I'll be fine now.'

The butler bowed his head. 'Then I wish you a pleasant meal.'

'I think that should be no problem,' said Anaïs.

The butler did an about-turn on the spot, his shoes squeaking on the polished floor, and left the room.

Anaïs watched him leave and then turned to survey the table. There was an enormous amount of food on it. Rows of steaming dishes were lined in front of her. There was a peculiar mix of smells. Salty fried bacon competed with the sweet waft of freshly cut fruit, the baked doughy odour of pancakes and the punchy pungency of aged cheese.

To her left, at the head of the table, the librarian appeared to have satisfied herself. She slouched in her chair and sipped a cup of coffee. Blowing across the black liquid to cool it, she looked over the cup at Anaïs and smirked.

'I could get used to this,' she said.

Anaïs rested her elbow on the table and cupped her

head in her hand. 'I'm sure you could. Remind me not to get too close to you next time you're eating. I wouldn't want to become part of the meal.'

Immi grunted at her but was too satisfied to muster a reply. Anaïs looked across the table at Nan.

The shade folded her arms and narrowed her eyes. *'Please eat something, Anaïs.'*

Anaïs wasn't particularly hungry. She never was. She reached out to the nearest plate and pulled it towards her. She selected a slice of pepperoni pizza. She nibbled on the crust but it wasn't to her liking and she discarded it. She hooked her hand around a dish of pitted green olives. She slid it under her chin and popped one into her mouth. They were good. She fed them into her mouth in one long, continuous flow, only pausing when the dish was empty.

The food made her lethargic. Her five-year-old body gave up on her. Her eyelids drooped and it required all her energy to keep them open.

'Nan,' she whimpered, 'I'm really tired.'

'Then sleep, Anaïs. You've done enough for one day.'

Anaïs yawned. 'Ok.'

She pushed the olive dish aside, folded her arms on the table and rested her head on them. Her eyelids fluttered and then shut. The last thing she heard before she fell asleep was the familiar snipe of the librarian.

'Wow! That's one heck of an after-meal dip.'

FOOD AND TRAINS AND TIME

Witches require very little food to survive. They can't do without it altogether, but a little goes a very long way. If anything, food is a symbolic thing associated with celebration. The witch metabolism is excellent at conserving energy. As everything about the physical growth of witches progresses at a leisurely pace, this should come as no surprise.

The fact that the dining table was so heavily laden had more to do with choice than anything else. If the scent or mere nibble of a piece of food is enough to sustain you for a day, then it's nice to have a wide variety of options to choose from.

In an emergency a witch can even conjure up a phantom smell to get her through the day. Naturals are also prone to this strange phenomenon, which has a fantastic name: phantosmia.

For naturals this affliction can be distressing and

unpleasant. Quite often these episodes are triggered by perfectly non-mysterious factors. Sometimes it is outside influences at play, but usually a natural's neurones are simply running rogue. The root cause stems from the brain. Like many other properties in the universe, witches have found a way to control this nasal sensory peculiarity.

Neurons are electrically charged nerve cells that send signals in the body. Astrocytes are star-shaped cells that provide the glue, connection, support and protection of neurons. Witches are able to harness the amazing cerebral superpower of astrocytes and redirect neurons at will. They do what most naturals do not. They put all that wasted space up there to good use.

The naturals among us who experience phantosmia perhaps have witch tendencies they are unaware of. There is, after all, a little bit of witch in everyone. Although witches can control their cerebral signals much more efficiently than naturals, and can invoke this sensation at will, the effect is not permanent. It will gradually wear off. It is not a satisfactory substitute for physical sustenance. Fast food chains have made a dubious science of something similar and use certain chemicals to trigger the opposite— recurring hunger. But we are getting off track here. Let us just sum it up by saying witches can stave off hunger, but not indefinitely.

On the subject of tracks, witches also encouraged the advancement of the railroad. Not merely so they could eat in comfort but in order to get around faster. Horses and other animals had previously been used, but, unfortunately, entities made of flesh and blood do not respond efficiently to magic. Every living thing has a mind of its own and controlling them requires a great deal of energy. Not only that, a restaurant looks slightly out of place when towed by a team of horses. As I have said before, attracting attention to yourself as a witch is not conducive to getting the job done.

Following the introduction of trains—and people took some convincing before they were readily accepted; beasts of iron and steel are scary things if you've never seen them before—witches had them stationed at strategic positions around the globe. The railway never would have become so widespread, and in such a short time, had it not been for the witch community.

Naturally, a witch train needs to have a few extras. If you are going to so much trouble, you might as well put magic to good use. Otherwise it would be a wasted opportunity. Thus the spectacular interior Anaïs had been confronted with. It should be noted that witches not only have private railway cars, but entire railroads. Over time these have become increasingly onerous to run and maintain. The main problem being: a railroad is a little difficult to conceal. They are just plain big. Not only that, they are complicated pieces of engineering. Unfortunately, real train systems cannot be broken down, folded up and put away in a box like a toy.

Witches not only maintain their own private lines, they also borrow public ones on occasion. Sometimes, you need to get your locomotive from one part of the world to another. You need the connections.

Unfortunately, increased traffic on existing railroad

networks has meant they have become incredibly congested. Often they cannot cope with what they already have. Throw a ghost train into the mix and you will surely create havoc. In general, witches have a knack for timing, so this is not necessarily a problem. But why make your life more difficult than it needs to be? The overriding reason witches use rail travel is for relaxation and recuperation. Keeping a strict timetable does not necessarily figure into the equation.

There has been one unfortunate by-product. Witch advancement in railways has had serious ramifications for the natural world. We now keep time by trains. Initially clocks had only one hand, a natural progression from the sundial. There was no need to count the minutes and seconds. Every town kept its own time. If you travelled to a neighbouring town there could be as much as an hour's difference in official time. In order for trains to operate efficiently, even witch trains, time had to be adjusted. It had to be standardised. If we go back a couple of centuries we will see that keeping time had less importance. Now we do more than just set our clocks by it. We set our entire lives according to the swing of a mechanical hand.

This advancement in timekeeping has not necessarily been a good thing. Now the entire world tries to fit itself into a regular schedule. There is even such a thing as Coordinated Universal Time.

If it had not been for a witch desire for comfort and mobile dining rooms we may not find ourselves now forced to live on a fictitious standardised time. We would be following the movement of the sun, which is the natural way of adjusting our inner clocks. Perhaps we would all feel a lot better for it.

Witches do not always make the correct choices but, thankfully, most naturals don't know this and have no idea who to blame.

TEENAGE DREAMS

naïs looked at her reflection in the mirror. It wasn't her. Partly it was, and partly not. She had changed and quite dramatically. She had aged. Curiously, it didn't bother her. She wondered why that was. Shouldn't she be freaking out? She wasn't. It was weird, the fact she didn't feel a thing, even stranger than the ageing thing. It left her cold, emotionless. As if it was normal, an everyday occurrence.

She studied her body and casually ran her eyes over its form. She guessed she was sixteen, maybe seventeen, certainly not five or six. Her hair was longer. It wasn't straight any more. Now it was wavy, the tips terminating in tight curls. It was a different colour, too. Blonde had darkened into brunette. She didn't like it. The first chance she got, she decided, she would hack it all off. Maybe she could do something radical with it. She toyed with the idea of dyeing it purple. She could shave it. Perhaps even a mohawk would look good. Whatever, it was too normal, too ordinary. She preferred extraordinary. Of course they wouldn't like that. The Organisation liked a smooth-running ship. Don't rock the boat, it might sink. No excesses, no anomalies, don't draw attention to yourself. If she went wild with her looks she would stand out and that wouldn't do. As a witch you had to blend in, be one of the crowd.

Her figure was different. No baby fat. She was long and slender. Everything was elongated. She didn't like it. Too many sharp edges. Even her face had changed. It wasn't round any more. It had stretched and her chin stuck out. She pulled some faces. She smiled and the dimples in her cheeks failed to appear. That was a shame. She liked them.

She stepped up to the mirror. She gently grabbed the corner of her mouth and gingerly tugged at her skin. It stretched taut over her cheekbones. She pushed and prodded it, leaving red spots on her face. Her eyes looked tired. They were way older than the rest of her body. They had seen too much. How old was she really? If she was physically in her late teens then mentally she would have to be forty, fifty or maybe even sixty. She bared her teeth. They looked pretty good. At least she hadn't lost any of them. She ran a finger along her incisors and poked around in her mouth. She went too deep. She choked and dry retched. It made her eyes water. She cleared her throat and swallowed. *Don't do that, you idiot.* She dried her wet finger on her leg.

What was going on? She couldn't have aged so much in one night. Not like this. That just didn't happen. It had to be a dream. She pinched her cheek. It didn't hurt. She was right. It *was* just a dream, a glimpse into the future. Only it was odd. Under normal circumstances her dreams were terrifying. In the past she'd had such vivid ones. Usually she was being chased by something or someone. She had doubts. She was confused. Maybe it wasn't a dream after all. She usually didn't know when they were happening.

The fact she felt no emotion whatsoever bothered her. Why was she being so nonchalant about it? Her body had transformed. She looked around the room. Maybe something would jump out of a cupboard or from under the bed and attack her. She raised her fists and took a boxer's stance. *C'mon, I'm ready! Give me your worst.*

She waited. Nothing. She exhaled slowly and dropped her shoulders. *Seems I'm in control here. Good, keep it that way.* She kept her fists up and swivelled around, running her eyes over the room again. *Stop this. Better not raise any demons.* She relaxed and let her arms fall. She shook them loose and flexed her legs. They were long. That felt good. No more puny baby legs. She felt like running. She jogged on the spot, pumping her knees. She stopped, breathing deeply, her heart pounding. *No, don't do that. Don't push it.*

She took one more look at her figure in the mirror. She could live with it. If that was how she was going to turn out, then it was acceptable. She hadn't put on heaps of weight or anything. It looked like she had kept fit. If she wanted to, she could do stuff to work on it, improve it. What a relief to have a body that could do so much more. Maybe that was why she wasn't concerned.

She climbed back into bed. It was warm under the covers. *Just go back to sleep.*

She closed her eyes and let images of her future self play through her head. Somehow it was comforting knowing that one day she would change. But there was no need to rush it. She should be content with who she was. The dream was showing her what she could become. She wouldn't be like that when she woke. She would still be baby Anaïs. She had heaps of time to grow. She was a witch, after all. She breathed in deeply, exhaled and let the shroud of darkness descend upon her.

BREAKFAST

Anaïs was astounded. 'A week! I slept for a week?'

'Yep,' said the librarian, drily.

'And what have you been doing?'

The librarian sighed and folded her arms. 'Going stir-crazy.'

'I can imagine.'

'No, I don't think you can,' said Immi, shaking her head. 'Can we please get out of here now?'

'I think you should eat something.'

Anaïs turned to the shade and looked at her with a dour face. 'I'm not hungry, Nan. I just woke up.'

Nan was insistent. *'Humour me. You need to have something. You've been asleep for a week.'*

Anaïs relented and dropped her shoulders. She knew better than to go up against her. The caretaker would never back down. 'Fine.'

She surveyed the dining table and yawned. She picked up a cocktail sausage and plunged it into a bowl of tomato sauce. She munched loudly on it. Anaïs looked across the table, her eyes flicking from one woman to the other. They both looked on with disdain.

She had woken a few moments earlier in a child's bed, her own bed, complete with princess canopy and all. In fact, the entire bedroom was an exact copy of her room in Amsterdam. Even the baby toys had been there. At first, Anaïs had been confused about where she was. She had stumbled to the door, rubbing sleep out of her eyes. She had opened the door and leaned on it, waiting a moment for her head to clear. Beyond the door was the landing at the top of the stairs in the entry hall. Above her, through the glass ceiling, the view outside was of a clear, bright-blue sky. She had screwed up her nose at it.

Anaïs had proceeded downstairs and found Nan and the librarian in the dining room. The nanny had greeted her with smiling eyes. The librarian had snarled at her. She had an inkling that she had been asleep for a long time, but was genuinely surprised when she found out how long it had actually been. She usually got by with catnaps and, once or twice a year, a full night's sleep. A week was out of proportion with her usual rhythm. Apparently, she had been more exhausted than she had first thought.

Anaïs finished the sausage and picked at her teeth with a fingernail. She stood at the table and looked across at the women. 'Who put me to bed?'

Nan's voice rang in her head. *'I did. Well, not completely on my own. The butler helped. You fell asleep at the table.'*

'Really? I must have been *really* tired.'

The cocktail sausages were good and she grabbed another one. She ploughed it into the bowl of sauce, shovelling a glob of it onto the sausage and dripping it over the table on the way to her mouth.

'Anaïs! Mind your manners.'

'Sorry,' she murmured through a mouthful of sauce and sausage.

The librarian tapped her foot impatiently. Anaïs finished eating. The librarian slid a napkin across the table. The little witch picked it up and wiped her face with it.

She eyed the women. 'Satisfied?'

The librarian shrugged and grunted.

'Not really, but I suppose it will have to do.' Nan walked around the table and knelt down beside her. *'How are you feeling?'*

Strangely the caretaker's face was at eye level. 'Fine,' said Anaïs. 'Why do you ask?'

'Oh, I was just wondering. Do you notice anything different about yourself?'

'Nope.'

'Look.' Nan pointed at her legs. Anaïs looked down.

She was dressed in a set of bright, purple pyjamas. They were her favourites. She scratched the back of her head. *How has all my stuff been transported from Amsterdam?* Even if it had somehow magically moved, it shouldn't exist. Everything would have been destroyed in the explosion. The train was full of surprises. Perhaps the butler could tell her.

The fact she was wearing her own pyjamas was one

thing, but not as unusual as the state they were in. There was something not quite right about them. They were uncomfortably tight, an extremely snug fit, and the pyjama legs only just reached below her knees. She looked at her sleeves. They were also undersized and barely covered her elbows. Had their magical transportation caused them to shrink? Or was it something else? Anaïs flushed with panic.

She looked frantically around the room. A full-length mirror hung on the wall next to the door. She dropped the napkin and rushed across to it. She stumbled as she moved. Her legs felt unsteady and the sudden movement made her light-headed. It took a moment to regain her balance and bring everything into focus. She stood in front of the mirror and stared at her reflection. Her jaw dropped. She had grown. And not just a little. A good twenty centimetres had been added to her height. She hadn't attained the age she had experienced in her dream, but had certainly made progress towards it.

Anaïs spun around and glared at the women. 'Why didn't you say anything?'

'Say anything? I'm surprised you didn't realise it when you woke up,' said Immi. 'There's no point telling you stuff like that. You wouldn't believe me anyway.'

Anaïs frowned at the nanny. 'Nan?'

'You just woke up. You're always grumpy when you wake up. If I'd said something before you were fully with it, you would have given me an earful.'

Anaïs eyed her. 'And what makes you think you won't get one now?'

Nan knew better than to get into an argument and bit her lip.

Anaïs looked at herself in the mirror again. 'Great! Now what?'

'We get out of here,' said the librarian.

'No,' said Anaïs, pulling at her pyjama front. 'Look at me. I'm huge! And my hair!' It too had grown and was a tangled mess, falling below her waist.

The librarian shrugged. 'Growth spurt, I guess? We checked on you yesterday and it'd already happened.'

Anaïs's voice rose in pitch. 'Weren't you surprised? Why didn't you wake me?'

'Surprised? You're a witch. What do I know? Maybe this is normal.' Immi flipped her thumb at the shade. 'She said to let you sleep. Not my choice. I would have preferred to get out of here.'

Anaïs scratched her head and looked first at Nan and then at the librarian. 'What? You can talk to her now?'

'No, not really.' The librarian looked at Nan. 'Show her.'

Nan stood up and walked across to the mirror. She frosted it with her breath. Using a finger, she drew her name in the ice crystals on the glass.

'Ingenious,' said Anaïs.

'I know, it was my idea,' said the librarian with a smug look on her face.

'I'm truly shocked,' said Anaïs. 'I never would have guessed you had that kind of brainpower.'

Nan cried out in her head. *'Anaïs!'*

The librarian folded her arms and glared at the witch.

'Anaïs, apologise! She's not so bad once you get to know her.'

Anaïs sighed and looked at the librarian. 'I'm sorry. My bad. It is very clever.'

The librarian eyed her and then decided the apology was reasonably genuine. 'Thanks, but I can't take all the credit. You've been asleep forever and we had a lot of time on our hands. Boredom can do strange things to your head. We didn't do it alone. We had a little help from the butler.'

As if on cue, the butler walked into the room balancing a huge cake on his gloved hands. He set it down on the dining table and pulled a box of matches out of his pocket.

Immi grinned at Anaïs. 'By the way, happy birthday!'

GROWTH SPURT

Not only child witches, but all children, have moments of immense growth. They can go to bed and, after a good night's sleep, get up the next morning transformed. There are usually telltale signs that this will occur. Quite often pain is involved. There will be cramps, legs will ache and such. If your body is going to stretch and suddenly explode on you, it's not surprising that it hurts.

Witches are prone to similar moments of exponential growth. However, as with most things in comparison with natural human beings, there are extremes.

In the first few years of human life, children tend to grow erratically. No two people grow at the same rate. One child will shoot up overnight while another will remain petite for years. Growth cycles are not an exact science and are generally very unpredictable. Even so, most children grow at an incredible rate.

Human development is similar to that of other

species. Youth is inevitably short. Held up against the amount of time we generally have on the planet, our formative years fly by. Yet the amount of physical growth in that short period is astounding.

Young children in particular have the most amazing jumps in growth. If you see them on a day-to-day basis this is not always obvious. Usually this is only apparent to the outsider. To the occasional visitor the physical changes can be truly shocking. These revelations are not always restricted to a visitor. A guardian or parent can experience the same. To those close to them there are moments when a child's sudden acceleration in physical development can be jaw dropping.

Overnight a child can grow several centimetres, or their facial features can completely transmogrify. In older children the change continues. Vocal cords can magically lower in tone, lumps of flesh appear where there were previously none. Their entire physique alters. The baby fat melts away, hips form and waists contract. Legs become slender and elongated. The skull, which starts off dimensionally out of balance, allows the rest of the body to catch up with it. The entire figure stops being a ball on a stick.

There is also the inevitable forest-like expansion of hair. In the case of manes, tresses and the humble fingernail this growth continues throughout life. Even death cannot stop it. Corpses have been documented sprouting the most incredible things. The human body is an unstoppable force when it comes to growth.

Witches are not immune to these peculiar physical idiosyncrasies. They are essentially human. The laws of nature apply to them in much the same way as to everyone else. Although their general process of ageing is torpid, they are also prone to the occasional growth spurt.

There is nothing especially magical about the transformations. In general, witches have a lot of catching up to do. Their bodies are constantly trying to find their natural age. There is very little known about what causes these sudden bodily changes, nor what prevents the usual standard rate of growth. Just as the human body remains a mystery, so it is with the physical shells of witches. Until they reach adulthood there are no certainties about what will occur. Even adult witches go through a variety of stages.

In her relatively short life, Anaïs had experienced a particularly abnormal rate of growth. As a baby she had grown very quickly. She had been able to walk at the age of three months and hold a lucid conversation at six. In the first two years of her physical existence, her rate of vertical expansion had been surprising. Then it had all stopped.

Except for the occasional minor spurt, her growth had stagnated. For over fifteen years she had been cursed with physical dimensions equivalent to those of a toddler. Nothing extraordinary had occurred to her physically. Anaïs had actually given up all hope of ever continuing to grow. She had accepted her lot as one of the vertically challenged.

Perhaps it had been the olives. Although this was improbable, she was particularly partial to them and it wasn't the first time she had devoured an entire bowl at one sitting. It was unlikely a nibble on a piece of pepperoni pizza had been the catalyst. Maybe food had nothing to do with it. Perhaps all she needed was a decent night's rest. That, she had certainly had.

Witches have an enormous capacity to just keep going. It has something to do with the amount of supernatural energy which surrounds them. Most people will require stimulants to keep going for days on end without proper rest. Witches are better off without extra chemical additives. They only cause havoc with their system and, in some cases, can be particularly harmful. Naturals also suffer from this. Human consumption of stimulants is legendary, but eventually there is a price to pay. You can party till you drop, but your body won't be thanking you.

This is not to say witches haven't dabbled in experimentation in order to prolong their waking hours. Sometimes, when you are on the job and must see it through to the bitter end, there'll not be the opportunity to take a break. Occasionally superior supernatural energy will not suffice. Even it has limits.

Apothecaries the world over have done their best to find safe analeptics. Some of these products have even found their way onto the open market. Unfortunately, some apothecaries also took the opportunity to earn a bit on the side. The Organisation clamped down hard on this behaviour, but even they cannot prevent the very human desire for consumerism. Greed is never an easy vice to control. Especially when the governments of the world continue to not only support, but encourage it.

Anaïs was not a consumer of stimulants. Yet she had

changed dramatically. As it was doubtful the pizza and olives contained magical properties, more than likely Anaïs was simply ready to grow. She had exhausted her toddler form. She needed room. Her physical self was automagically giving her the opportunity to expand. As she aged she would be required to do more with her talents. The universe would have to allow her to make full use of them. Trapping her physically was a barrier which could inhibit her reaching her full potential. As a witch she had more to do than most.

EIGHTEEN

Happy birthday? It was all too much for Anaïs. 'I have to sit down.'

The butler, who was about to light the candles on the cake, blew out the match in his hand. He pulled a chair out from the table. 'Take a seat, madam. And many happy returns.'

Anaïs grumbled, 'Thanks.' She sat down.

He went to push her in. She waved him away. 'Just … just … Oh leave it.'

'As you wish.' The butler released the chair, walked around the table and lit a fresh match. He began to light the candles. Anaïs sat and watched him, brooding in silence. The cake stood in the centre of the table in front of her. The butler moved meticulously from one candle to another, keeping his hand cupped around the match as he went. The candlelight flickered on her sullen face.

Nan made an attempt to cheer her up. *'Anaïs, you should be happy. It's your birthday.'*

'Birthday, pfff … Who cares? This is too weird.

Most people celebrate turning a year older. I just aged three.' She stretched her arms and looked at them. 'At least, I think I physically aged three years. Maybe more. Who in the world has a birthday like that?'

Nan sat down beside her. *'I thought you would be happy. An eight-year-old body is an improvement on that of a five-year-old. You were always complaining about being so small.'*

Anaïs folded her arms, slid them onto the table and rested her chin on her forearms. 'I'm still small.' She flexed her fingers and scrutinised the back of her hand. 'Just not as small as I once was.' She reached out and drew a circle on the table with her index finger. 'I guess I need some time to adjust.'

'I understand. It's a shock for me as well. Another big change. But we'll get through it. We've had to deal with worse things in the past.'

'Yes, I know, you're right.' Anaïs leaned back, turned and gave her a smile. 'I'm just a bit worried about what will happen next. Who knows what's possible? I could go to sleep and wake up in the body of a sixty-year-old or something.'

'Just don't sleep,' said the librarian.

Anaïs rolled her eyes. 'You're not helping.' She shot the librarian a stern look. 'If you don't have something constructive to say, then don't bother saying anything at all.'

The librarian raised her hands in mock defence. 'Sheesh!'

The butler finished lighting the candles, blew out the match in his hand and stood back to admire his handiwork.

'I doubt you will age that quickly, Anaïs, but I suppose anything is possible. I'm as much in the dark as you are. Maybe we should see if we can find someone who knows more about this sort of stuff?'

'Yes, I think that would be a good idea.' She bit her bottom lip and sniffed. 'Right now, I'm feeling a bit lost. We need help.'

The librarian picked up a wicked looking carving knife from the table and flicked the blade with her fingernail. The metal pinged. 'Cake anyone?'

Anaïs shot her another steely glance and snapped at her. 'You really have no empathy, do you?'

'Empathy? I have empathy.' The librarian was genuinely insulted. She waved the knife at Anaïs. 'You stress too much. Get over it. Hurry up and blow out the candles. The icing is melting.'

The train swung unexpectedly from one side to the other, reminding them they were in a moving vehicle. The librarian lost her footing and dropped the knife. It clanged on the floor. She dodged the blade as it bounced and grabbed the edge of the table with both hands for support. Anaïs did the same, her knuckles showing white. The train abruptly slowed, sending everything on the table sliding to one end. Fortunately, the table's raised bevelled edge prevented everything from ending up on the floor. Even so, the butler swept around the table and assumed a catcher's stance. He relaxed once the vehicle had settled into a slower pace. He looked around at the others in the room, stood up and self-consciously smoothed the front of his jacket.

'Whoa!' exclaimed Immi. She steadied herself with the table. 'Someone needs driving lessons.'

'I do believe we have arrived at our destination,' announced the butler.

'Great, let's get out of here,' said the librarian.

Anaïs stopped her, 'Just a moment.'

She stood and pushed her chair back. 'I'm still going to have a piece of this.' She eyed the cake with determination. 'No matter what stupid physical form I take, I'm only going to be eighteen once.'

She took a deep breath, held it for a moment and blew out all the candles in one go.

THE HUNTING LODGE

The hunting lodge sat on the shore of a man-made lake and was surrounded by thick forest. It had the proportions of a castle and even all the prerequisites for one. There was no moat, but a high stone wall surrounded its internal structure. A collection of buildings encircled an expansive courtyard. A disproportionately tall and slender square tower rose from the centre of the largest building and jutted out from it like an afterthought. Its extreme dimensions set it out of kilter with the rest of the property. If it had been circular in form it would have looked exactly like a rocket with its spire-shaped roof. Standing in the open gates and looking up, he pondered whether the tower was actually some form of escape conveyance.

Even though the lodge was in the middle of open countryside, and the only structure on the expansive property, it had a number: 258. Presumably post had to be delivered somewhere. In order for that to occur, there needed to be a post box, an address. Nevertheless, he doubted whether a mailman would have the gall to approach such a strange building. It wasn't exactly inviting. But that could have just been his own impression. He was there to face the music for what had happened.

He proceeded through the gates and across the courtyard. Heading towards the main building, he walked through the shadow cast by the tower. A chill ran through him and he shivered. The winter sun was weak but had at least provided a glimmer of warmth. The steel and glass awning protruding out of the building, and above its front door, looked as if it had been stolen from another structure. It looked like the entrance to a train station. Maybe the structure was indeed a launch pad.

As he approached the entrance the heavy, wooden front door swung open. He was expected, although nobody stood there to greet him. A guide was unnecessary. He knew the way. It wasn't the first time he had been summoned to the main house, but it had never been under such circumstances. This time he would need to make excuses. He had failed the task. They would be seeking answers he doubted he could provide.

With some trepidation he stepped into the building and stood for a moment in the entry hall. Behind him he heard the door close with a click. The tiled ceiling hung forebodingly above him. Its bulk and form pressed down upon him and made the space feel smaller than it was. A rogue thought ran through his mind. *Who had designed this odd place? And why on earth would anyone want to tile a ceiling?*

To his left a sculpture of an owl, carved in dark

wood, sat on the balustrade at the foot of a set of steep stairs. The jewels embedded in the centre of its eye sockets winked at him. He avoided their gaze.

He continued along the hallway and stood before a set of heavy carved double doors. Next to them another sculpture, this one cast in bronze, towered over him. It was an impressionistic depiction of an eagle and stood on a low pedestal. It dominated the narrow corridor. Its size and polished metal beak were menacing.

The doors swung open and, with some hesitation, he stepped into the next room. He lifted his hand to shelter his eyes from the glare of a row of gigantic windows. Somehow their form also reminded him of the sash windows on a train, only larger. Cutting across the room between himself and the windows was a long, wooden table with tiles embedded in its top. A row of high backed chairs lined the far side of the table. Seated in them were several men with terse looks on their faces. On his side of the table was a solitary chair.

'Sit down, Ignatius,' said the man seated at the centre of the table.

The Inquisitor breathed in deeply. He hated it when his father used his full name.

MONT SAINT-MICHEL

The railway station was in a state of total disrepair. Water ran in rivulets down the walls and the whole place had the salty stench of the ocean. In fact, the entire tunnel looked as if it had just been drained of water. Algae grew in every crevice. Crustaceans had ensconced themselves in the brickwork and everything glistened like an underwater cavern. The only thing it lacked was fish.

The conductor helped Anaïs down onto the platform. She was somewhat unsteady on her feet and still getting used to her eight-year-old legs. The ground seemed so far away all of a sudden. It didn't help that the platform was scattered with loose tiles, the mortar under them having crumbled to powder. A rotting wooden sign secured with rusted bolts was attached to the wall in front of her. It declared their destination in faded lettering:

MONT SAINT-MICHEL

Anaïs looked up at the conductor.

'Thank you,' she said.

She studied his face, trying to adjust to the fact she wasn't talking to his brother, the butler, any more. She turned her attention to the station itself and looked around her. 'Where are we?'

'We are in France, miss. Directly across the Channel from our port of embarkation.'

Anaïs raised an eyebrow. 'Oh, ok.' She waved her arm down the platform. 'What happened here?'

'I fear very little has happened, miss.' He studied the walls and seemed almost as perplexed as she was. 'We haven't made the trip in quite some time. However, I have to admit I am as confused as you. The station should be better maintained.'

'How long is "quite some time"?'

'Years, I suppose.' He pulled off his cap and scratched his forehead. 'I'm afraid I couldn't tell you for certain. We used to be very busy, but things have changed. I have no idea why.'

'Perhaps your passengers prefer to fly nowadays,' said Anaïs.

'No, I don't think so,' said the conductor. 'They always flew, so that can't be it. Maybe they just don't have the time. We are not the fastest mode of transport, you know. Although, having said that, my brother is quite capable of getting a fair rate of knots out of *The Devil*. '

Anaïs made a mental calculation in her head. 'England can't be that far from here. It took us at least a week. We did it before in less time with a small boat.'

'I realise that, miss, but it was for your benefit. We are quite capable of doing the trip in a few hours if necessary.'

Anaïs was surprised. 'Oh, I just thought ….'

He smiled at her. 'I understand perfectly. It is your first trip. Next time we will make better time if necessary.'

'Good to know,' said Anaïs. 'I'm sorry to hear you don't get a lot of passengers. I enjoyed my trip. Perhaps there are just more flights than there were a few years ago? The skies are crammed with aircraft.'

'I am fully aware of that,' said the conductor. 'Although, I do have to admit it has been quite some time since I've gone to the surface.'

'Really? You never get out? You stay here in the tunnel?'

'Of course! We are on standby for every emergency, big or small.' He puffed out his chest proudly. 'We are here to serve. Unfortunately, I think my brother has been slacking off.' A look of concern clouded his face and he inspected the floor. He flipped a loose tile over with the point of his polished boot. 'The station is in a disgraceful state.'

'Do you mean your brother, the engineer? It's not his fault if he's stuck at the other end of the line.'

'Oh, no, he has enough to do. This is not his job.' The conductor swept his hand around the tunnel. 'My other brother, the stationmaster, takes care of this.'

Anaïs rolled her eyes and snorted. 'Naturally!'

She quickly covered her mouth, realising it wasn't a laughing matter. Maybe the man was dead. If the train hadn't made the trip in many years anything could have happened. She suddenly felt sorry for the conductor.

'One moment, miss,' said the conductor. He stepped to the middle of the platform and cupped his hands around his mouth. He called out, 'Hergé? Where are you?'

There was a moment of silence. It was punctuated by a deafening blast. A jet of steam shot from the locomotive and filled the platform. Anaïs jumped in surprise at the sound. The engine hissed its boiler empty and once again silence prevailed. A shrill voice followed, emanating from the far end of the platform. 'Ok, ok, I'm coming. Hold your horses!' It was accompanied by the sound of a walking stick clacking on the tiles.

Emerging out of the steam at the head of the train an incredibly wizened old man hobbled towards her. Except for his age, he was the spitting image of the other members of the train staff. He was hunched over a short, crooked walking stick. An immaculate, ivory-white beard flowed down his body. It tapered to a point and glowed starkly in the dimly lit tunnel. The tip of it almost touched the ground.

Anaïs turned to thank the conductor but he had vanished. The old man gave her no time to consider his disappearance. He stopped next to the locomotive, the steam dissipating around his legs, and waved her over to him. 'Right this way, missy. I have no desire to escort you all the way to the lift.'

'Lift?' The librarian climbed down from the carriage.

Anaïs couldn't rid herself of her curiosity. 'Did you see the conductor?'

The librarian raised an eyebrow. 'There was a conductor?'

Anaïs was more confused than ever.

THE LIFT

They clambered into the lift. There was barely enough room for all of them and Nan brushed up against Immi. She shivered and shrank away from the shade's cold touch.

'Give me a bit of room, why don't you,' she hissed through gritted teeth.

Anaïs looked at her ruefully. 'It would help if you didn't insist on wearing so much clothing.'

The librarian pulled her enormous fluffy coat tightly around her and hunched her shoulders. 'I'm cold.'

'Still …' began Anaïs.

'Now, ladies, let's have a little calm in here,' said the stationmaster. He gave them a stern look. He flicked his beard over his shoulder like a scarf and squeezed in between them. He turned and slammed the lift's elaborately decorated wrought-iron scissor door shut. They all cringed as it screeched loudly on its rusted metal runners. He turned a key in the door and latched it. He rattled the door to make sure it was secure.

The lift was ancient, dating back to the 1890s. It had mirrored walls, which were speckled with age and barely offered any reflection. Plush red velvet was fixed to the ceiling with studs like a seat cushion. The stationmaster forced his way between the women with a plethora of 'sorry's'. Crammed in shoulder to shoulder, there was not enough room. They shuffled as one in an anti-clockwise direction to allow him access to the lift's control console. He made some space for himself and, standing in front of a giant brass L-shaped lever, planted his foot on a button coming out of the floor. He straightened, cracking his back. Using both hands he pulled the lever towards him and cranked it to one side. The numbers zero, one, two and three were embossed on a brass plate behind it. The stationmaster slotted the lever into three.

A whirring came from above. The lift shuddered and began its ascent. Metal grated on metal, emitting a high-pitched screech and causing the women to clap their hands around their ears. It rocked violently to one side, throwing them off balance. They all searched in vain for something to hold. The stationmaster steadied himself against the lever.

'Sheesh,' yelled the librarian above the din.

Mercifully, the squealing and scraping of metal gradually ceased as the lift accelerated. It rumbled along on its runners, gently swaying from side to side. Through the door they could watch their ascent. Layers of sedimentary rock flashed by. It was as if they were travelling up from the bowels of the earth. The dank, salty smell of the railway station receded as they climbed higher.

The journey seemed to last forever. No one spoke. They shot silent, furtive glances at each other. The stationmaster ignored them and gazed at the rock face flitting by. He played with his beard and munched on his dentures. Anaïs studied him, still trying to work out if she had been dealing with a set of brothers or one person in different guises.

As the rock changed colour to a reddish brown he pulled the lever towards him, turned it and slotted it into the number two position. The lift slowed. Rock gave way to wooden panelling and the stationmaster repositioned the lever into one. The lift crawled the last few metres, revealing first a floor and then a room. The stationmaster slotted the lever into zero.

Using a button on the wall he inched the lift up until its floor was perfectly level with the floor of the room. He unlatched the scissor door and slid it open, skilfully retracting his fingers at the last moment so as not to get them caught between door and frame. It slammed loudly into the housing recessed into the frame. The stationmaster stepped out into the room and moved to one side to allow the women to exit. One by one they got out. Now released from the tight confines of their iron coffin, they stretched and shook themselves.

Anaïs looked around the bare room. Except for a solitary wooden stool there was nothing noteworthy. The stationmaster directed their attention to a door at the far end of the room. 'Your car is waiting downstairs. I do hope you had a pleasant journey.' He attempted a cordial smile but his dentures nearly fell out. He jammed them up into the roof of his mouth, did an about-turn and re-entered the lift. The women watched him descend before turning to the door.

'After you,' said Anaïs to the librarian.

'Oh, no,' she replied and shook her head. 'I insist.' She swept an arm towards the door. She tilted her head and gave the little witch a sarcastic smile. 'After you, Anaïs. Birthday girl first.'

THE BALLROOM

Tentatively, Anaïs cracked the door open and peeked through to an enormous hall. Tall windows lined one wall and ran floor to ceiling. Intense morning sunlight flooded through them. It threw bright rectangles upon the dark, polished wooden floor. She cast her eyes around the hall. Dusty chandeliers hung from the ceiling, which was vaulted and decorated with frescos. It looked like a ballroom waiting to be filled with dancers. Although it was silent, Anaïs could almost hear the resonating sound of an orchestra playing and imagine the room filled to bursting with partygoers.

Anaïs stepped through the doorway and walked out into the centre of the hall. Just like the room she had left, it was devoid of furniture. The walls were lined with portraits of generations of noblemen and women. Long, tattered banners hung from rails that skirted the ceiling. Although there was a layer of dust on everything, an amazing conglomeration of colour jumped out from the walls.

Nan and Immi moved into the hall. The door clicked shut behind them. Anaïs turned to look and it took her a moment to find it. The door had virtually disappeared. Disguised as part of the wall, it was embedded in wooden panelling and skilfully hidden in full view.

The librarian assessed the room and chewed on her lower lip. 'Impressive,' she said and put her hands on her hips.

'Yes, it's quite something,' said Anaïs. 'Shall we keep moving?'

The librarian nodded and led the way towards double doors at the far end of the hall. Anaïs followed her and stopped when she realised Nan hadn't moved. She pulled her sunglasses out of the beret and put them on. She looked at Nan. The caretaker stood in awe, gaping at the ceiling.

'Nan?'

The nanny reluctantly pulled her gaze away from the ceiling and looked at the little witch. *'Oh, sorry Anaïs. I was just having a look, reminiscing. Sometimes it's nice to stop. You know, take a moment and have a good look around at your surroundings.'*

'Yes, you're right,' said Anaïs. 'We don't do that enough.'

'It's a beautiful room. They must have had the most fabulous parties here.'

'Yeah. You know what? I was thinking exactly the

same thing. I could almost hear them when I entered.' She moved into one of the sunlit rectangles on the floor. The warmth of the winter sun recharged her. She looked up at the portraits on the wall and grinned. 'Echoes of the past, eh Nan? Grand ball gowns and servants and all that stuff. How wonderful it must have been.'

Nan flashed her a wicked smile. *'Yes, and how very decadent.'*

Anaïs smiled back and then frowned. 'Times have changed, though.'

'Indeed, times have changed. But it doesn't have to be that way.' She folded her arms. *'We could throw our own party. We used to do that, just the two of us, remember?'*

Anaïs nodded.

'It's your birthday. We should dance.'

Anaïs shook her head. 'Oh no, don't be silly. We don't have to do that.'

'Why not? It's not like you to refuse an offer to dance. Or do you only dance in front of the mirror in your bedroom?'

Anaïs coloured red. 'How do you know that?'

'I have eyes and ears.'

Anaïs looked around the room. The librarian had stopped at the double doors and was waiting for them. She tapped her foot impatiently.

Nan stepped into her line of sight. *'Don't worry about her. She can wait.'* The shade offered her a hand. Anaïs took it and stepped in close. She stiffened and resisted the urge to shiver. She looked into the nanny's eyes.

The caretaker held her by the shoulders and out at arm's length. *'Wow, you really have grown.'*

'Yeah, it's weird,' said Anaïs. 'And you used to be so much bigger.'

Nan grinned at her. *'You used to be so much smaller.'* She pulled Anaïs into a waltz position and dipped her head. *'Ready? One, two, three.'*

They set off together, launching themselves with one great stride. They spun around the room. Both of them broke into laugher. The witch's shoes squeaked on the floor as she twirled around. The sound of the shoes and laughter echoed loudly in the cavernous room.

The librarian stood with one hand on a doorknob and watched them with a sour look on her face.

Anaïs stepped out of Nan's embrace. She skipped around the circumference of the room. She moved into the centre of the hall and stopped. She attempted a pirouette and almost fell. Throwing back her head she yelled at the ceiling in delight. 'Happy birthday to me!'

Her voice resonated back down at her from above. It bounced off the walls and ran around the room just as she had done. The dusty portraits on the wall glared down sternly at her. She poked her tongue out at them.

The librarian shook her head. 'Shhhh,' she hissed.

Anaïs shrugged and held up her arms. 'What?'

'Quiet,' said Immi. 'Someone might hear you.'

'I don't care.' Anaïs waved her arm dismissively up at the portraits. 'And it's not like they're going to mind. I'm sure they're grateful for some entertainment.'

The librarian looked up at the faces. She eyed them suspiciously, half expecting one of them to jump down off the wall. 'I didn't mean them.'

Anaïs huffed and dropped her arms at her sides. 'Fine, we'll go.'

She walked over to the nanny and grabbed both her hands. A chill shot up her arms but Anaïs held them firmly. She looked the shade squarely in the eye. 'Thanks, Nan, I needed that. I'm so glad you're here.'

'Me too, Anaïs,' said Nan, her eyes glinting through her camouflage. *'I wouldn't want to be anywhere else.'*

MAINLAND

The French namesake of their place of departure was a good deal larger than its British counterpart. Anaïs exited the ballroom and walked out onto a large balcony. It was bordered by a waist-high stone parapet. She peered over the edge and medieval buildings fanned out beneath her. Unlike the island in Cornwall, this one housed more than just a fortress. It was also a town. Ancient houses were stacked up on one another. They tumbled down the hill below the little witch. Crooked, narrow streets sliced their way with irregularity between the buildings.

The town was one thing. More startling to Anaïs was the view beyond the island—if it could be called an island. It appeared to be encircled not by the sea, but by sand. It stretched as far as she could see. There were odd patches of water but for the most part, everything was white, almost as if they were on an island in the middle of a desert.

Anaïs walked along the balcony that skirted the

ballroom. She followed the line of the parapet. The view changed as she rounded a corner. There was a shoreline. A minuscule strip of green ran along the horizon. A perfectly perpendicular line connected the island to the horizon—a road. Anaïs followed the line of the road towards her and dropped her eyes. Closer to her there was sand on either side of it. The expanse of sand was broken up by great pools of water. The road was actually some form of causeway. Far below her, a movement caught her attention. A small black dot moved slowly across a wide swathe of concrete at the base of the island. It was like a small beetle crawling across an enormous flat rock. The black dot stopped where the road joined the island. Anaïs squinted at it. Even though it was far away she could make out a familiar shape. It was the Morris Minor.

The librarian stepped up beside Anaïs. She looked over the edge of the parapet and spotted the car.

'Good,' she said. 'We can get out of here. Come on, let's go.'

Immi walked across the balcony and through a stone archway. She began to descend a set of stairs. Her heels clacked on the stone. A gust of cold wind swept across the balcony and whipped Anaïs's jacket around her legs. She turned the collar up and pulled it snug around her neck.

Nan's voice sounded in her head. *Yes, come on Anaïs, let's go.*

The caretaker went after the librarian. Anaïs hesitated.

Standing on the balcony she felt exposed yet

somehow safe. She looked behind her at the solid stone walls that rose up around her. She tilted her head back. They towered high above her and made her feel smaller than she actually was. *Go? Why should I go?* For a moment she considered staying where she was. She could even get back on the train. Why tempt fate by going somewhere else? She could hide. She didn't really need the promptuary. She could camp out in the fortress like a hermit for a while. Maybe in a few years she would grow some more—physically grow, so she could deal with whatever was expected of her. She knew she had responsibilities as a witch, but there were other witches. She wasn't the only one. Someone else could fill in for a while. She needed time to adjust to who she was. More than that, she needed to understand *what* she was.

'Anaïs, you can't stay here.'

Nan's soft voice took her by surprise. It also bothered her. Why couldn't she keep her head to herself? She closed her eyes and frowned. 'Why not?'

'Because I said so.'

'I'm afraid that's not enough of a reason for me.'

'Then do it for me, Anaïs. I'm still here for a reason. You have to help me.'

Anaïs had not considered that Nan was like other shades. Someone who needed her help. The caretaker had always been there to help *her*, not the other way around. She owed Nan big time, much more than any other shade she was ever likely to come across. Anaïs opened her eyes and looked around the balcony. She was surprised to see Nan standing in the archway at the far end. She had assumed the shade had gone ahead.

The thought struck her that maybe Nan couldn't go anywhere without her. Maybe they were intrinsically linked. Maybe they were inseparable.

'Come on, Anaïs.' Nan flicked her head, indicating they should go. *'Let's keep moving and find a way to fix your handbook. Maybe once that's done we can take a break, have a proper rest for a while. Let's just do this and then we'll see.'*

Anaïs twisted her lip. 'I suppose you're right.' She smiled at the shade and nodded slowly. 'Ok, I'll do it, but only because of you, Nan.'

The caretaker shook her head. *'I am not important, Anaïs. Although, it's reassuring to know you feel that way. You have responsibilities. Unfortunately, we all do. Sometimes we just have to do what we are supposed to do.'*

Anaïs took a deep breath. 'Nan, I get what you're saying but I don't want to think about them—the responsibilities.' She walked across the balcony and stood in front of the shade. 'I'm still doing it for you and I can't be bothered discussing it. Let's just go.'

She took Nan's arm in her own. Together they wound their way down through the tight network of streets in the village. Oddly, it was entirely deserted. At the base of the island they walked out through a narrow doorway and onto the concrete area Anaïs had seen from above. The Morris Minor stood parked before her, in the middle of the road leading from the island. Anaïs looked back at the town rising up behind her. She was slightly perplexed as to where the car had come from. There were no openings wide enough in the stone wall circling the base of the medieval structure. But then, there was so much that was unexplained. She decided not to dwell on it. The car was there. That was important. Without the promptuary to provide information, the Morris Minor was the only guide they had.

As she approached it, the car seemed to look up at her with its doe-eyed headlights and follow her movements. The librarian was leaning against the driver's door, arms folded across her chest.

'Why does everything always take so long with you?' she said with irritation.

Anaïs shrugged. 'I'm in no hurry. Are you?'

The librarian considered her for a moment. 'I like to keep moving. I feel safer that way.'

Anaïs cocked her head. 'Why? Is there something you're afraid of?'

'Not exactly, but I prefer to keep one step ahead. Since I've met you, we've run into some pretty strange things. Avoidance is the best defence.'

'Maybe it's safer not to move then, especially if we keep running into things.'

'No,' said the librarian shaking her head. 'We did that as well and then things started running into us. Don't you remember?'

'I remember,' said Anaïs, recalling the moment the Inquisitor's four-wheel-drive had collided with them in Cornwall. The librarian was correct. A medieval fortress was not going to offer any protection if someone really wanted to find her. She needed stronger magic, and only the promptuary could provide that. They would have to keep going until they found a solution to its problems.

The librarian lifted her head towards the fortress. 'Did you have fun up there?'

'What do you mean?'

'Your little ballroom experience.'

'As a matter of fact, yes we did. You should dance more often. It helps.'

The librarian raised an eyebrow. 'I'll try to remember that. What's the plan?'

'Get out of here?'

'Yes, I know that. What about a destination?'

'Don't look at me. The book's broken. At least, I think it is. Maybe I should check.'

'Maybe you should,' said the librarian.

Anaïs felt around in her beret and pulled out the promptuary. The star on its cover winked dully at her. She opened it. Its pages were unchanged.

She dropped it back in her beret and shook her head. 'Nope, it's not working.' She looked at the Morris Minor. 'We haven't got much choice. I hope this little car knows what it's doing. It's the only magic we've got.'

The librarian fixed her with a grim stare. 'So do I, Anaïs, so do I.'

DIFFERENT

A major problem with the world is many people think that different is wrong. They are wrong. Different is good.

If everything were a clone of everything else, where would we be? The world would certainly be a far less interesting place to live. It's all those discrepancies, oddities and variety that make life fun. Ok, I suppose for some it's not fun. People yearn for something better than they already have. Better won't always provide peace of mind, though. It's like having the powers of a witch. It's a nice thing to possess, all that wonderful magic, but it doesn't come for free. Even witches need to work at what they have. Not that their magic will be completely taken away if it's not put to good use. However, as with all special skills, there is the danger their abilities will waste away through neglect.

In the same way that a motor that hasn't been fired up for a long time needs time to warm up, or a seed that has been reduced to a dried-out husk needs to soak in water before it will sprout, we have to nurture our abilities before there is progress. The risk is if we wait too long it will become more and more difficult to do anything with what we have been given. It will require a lot of energy to get those abilities up and running.

Exercise and experimentation are necessary to give a gift the chance to surface and reach full capacity. Waiting around for something to happen will not bring results. You have to work at it. Everyone needs to put effort into the search for their particular form of different. Witches are there to help you find it but, at the same time, they are also grappling with their own abnormalities.

Anaïs didn't *want* to be different. She had been born with her difference. Difference had been thrust upon her. Ideally, she'd have tried to avoid her special complication. For a certain period of her short life she had been relatively successful at this. But ideal worlds do not exist. All along she had wanted to blend in, to be like everyone else, to be normal. Alas, she could not.

Is there such a thing as normal anyway? Even for non-witches?

No matter how different we are, we all have something worthwhile to do. This part of being different is especially important. All of us, not just witches, possess a special skill. Magic is everywhere. We are the creators of it. If we don't do what we should be doing we break the system. It is our responsibility to do what we are good at, even beyond death. And even if it makes us different.

Anaïs had doubts, but with good cause. She did not

know exactly what it was she needed to do to make her gift work properly. Her special kind of different was not like everybody else's. What set her apart was her incredibly crucial role in the universe. Like other witches her task was to make sure those who had not found their own special skill or who had not exercised it were given the opportunity to do so. Her goal was to make 'different' work for everyone. That was *her* gift, her special skill. Unfortunately, it had not come with an instruction manual. And the only thing she had that came close to a manual was in a state of disrepair.

BACK INTO THE FIELD

His training had been extensive but he had lacked enough real-world experience. That was what he had told them. He had foundered, like a fish out of water, and it bothered him. They had sent him out without a mentor which had made his job nigh impossible. Being sent out alone was foolish, but times were difficult. Cost-cutting measures had been their excuse. He cursed them for it. As far as he was concerned, lame excuses didn't cut it. He had not been fully prepared and they should have known that.

Getting sucked into a vortex and funnelled through a portal is no stroll in the park. It doesn't occur without leaving some lingering scarring, which didn't necessarily have to be physical. It had scared the hell out of him and undermined his confidence. And now they had told him to get on with it.

Yeah right!

He stood in front of the bathroom mirror and examined his eyes. He ran a finger along the lines running under them. He noted how bloodshot his eyes were and how they had aged tremendously. Yet the rest of his face was unaltered. He looked as young as ever. Perhaps too young for his age. Only his eyes betrayed him. He felt old because of them. He rubbed them and looked again. Nothing had changed. He cupped his hands and dipped them into the water in the basin. It was cold but invigorating. He threw the water up onto his face and fumbled blindly for a hand towel.

What he felt was not the fluffy linen he expected. The strands were much longer. He swiftly retracted his hand and wiped his face with his sleeve. For a moment he didn't dare look. He took a deep breath. The smell of brimstone seared his nostrils. He opened his eyes and looked down. The dog was back.

He had secretly hoped to be rid of it. No such luck. The bitter taste of the ash cloud rising from its hindquarters caused him to choke. He opened the tap and stuck his lips under the flow. He swished water around his mouth and spat it out. He looked down at the animal. Its bright red eyes stared back up at him. He sighed. Fine. At least he knew where he stood, knew what assistance he had. But it hadn't helped him before. Whatever had attacked them had been stronger than the pair of them. It had special powers. He should keep his distance.

Only… Where was it? The thing that had sent them through the vortex. This disturbed him. It could be watching them right now. At the time he'd thought he had died. He imagined death would be that way—a bright, white light and then darkness. That is what everyone said death would be like. When it had happened, he'd believed it was over. He had perished, gone on to another world. The magic, or whatever it was, had sent him somewhere dark. When light returned he'd been surprised, but relieved, to find himself still alive. He had been even more perturbed when he'd realised he was a vast distance from where he needed to be.

He knew by the time he managed to get back to where he had been, it would be too late. Their scent would have been transported away with them, gone cold. He had mulled it over and decided to change tactic. Next time he would concentrate on following the girl. The council had agreed. She was special. He had not known it at first, busy as he'd been following the old man. The shade had been his focus, not the girl. She was not the target. She had just been the bait that led him to the dead guy. It was not part of his protocol to confront the living anyway. He was sent out to bury the dead. And to bury them forever.

He began to question why he was doing it. Were they both working towards the same end, the girl and him? No, that couldn't be. She had been protecting the shade. His job was to make sure no one saw the dead. Shades had to be put to rest, kept in the shadows. He had the tools to do that, and that was his responsibility. The only problem was, she had been standing in the way.

It angered him that he had been so fixated on the old man. He cursed himself for not being more aware of his surroundings. *Stupid!* Had he kept his eyes open he would have spotted whatever it was that had sent him into the vortex.

Who was the little girl anyway? It was clear that she was in disguise. Under the skin she was a lot older than she looked. It was a good camouflage. If she hadn't been so animated, if he hadn't been able to see her expressions, he might have taken her for a shade. She wasn't, though. She was something else altogether. She was definitely alive. How she masked herself was a mystery to him. He had seen many strange things in his time, but this was different. *She* was different. He had never come across anyone protecting the dead.

How far should he go to get his job done? He had no directive to kill the living. He was meant to do the exact opposite. He was there to preserve life by preventing the dead from coming back. There were too many of them already. He couldn't detect them all. It was hard enough, without one of the living getting in the way.

Maybe he could leverage her knowledge. Apparently she could see them. If he shadowed her she would lead him to more of them. Then he could send the hound in. It could hold them. That's what it was for. Once it had captured them he could send them on to wherever it was they went. It was not his concern where that was. That was someone else's job. He was only one part of the machine, one link in the chain. It didn't concern him what the others did. He focussed on his job. That was all he could do. Just make the quota; more, if possible.

They hadn't been happy. *Damn them,* he thought, *I know what I'm doing. How would they like to do my job?* It's easy to criticise from behind a desk, but he was the one out in the field. He was the one in the firing line. They could have provided more assistance. Then his job could be done more effectively. His aspirations were high but his main drive was doing good. They knew that as well as he did. It was not good to have a world with all those shades running around freely. They could not be let loose and allowed to terrorise the population.

A buzzer sounded and a light flashed on a telephone mounted on the wall next to the mirror. He pressed the speaker button.

'Yes?'

A male voice squelched. 'We need to speak to you again.'

The Inquisitor breathed deeply. 'Fine, I'll be there. Just give me a moment, please.'

The speaker clicked and there was silence.

They wanted to talk to him again. *What was it this time?* He knew what he had to do. Even if they were not going to provide more assistance, he required no further instructions.

'Ask no questions.' That's what they had said. 'Can you keep an open mind and ask no questions?'

'Yes,' he had replied. 'It's what I always do.'

He prided himself on his professionalism. Not everyone could stomach the job. Not everyone could focus on what needed to be done. Not everyone was so efficient. That's why he had been given the job. He was trustworthy, and if he chose to do something he stuck it out to the bitter end. He had demonstrated his dedication. And, by god, he was not going to waver from it.

OVERLAND

A naïs lay across the back seat of the Morris Minor, her head in Nan's lap. She used her coat both as a pillow and a layer of protection. Had she not done this, lying with her head directly on the shade's icy body would have given her the mother of all brain freezes.

The librarian sat in the driver's seat and let the Morris Minor do its job. Anaïs watched Immi's eyes dart back and forth as the road flew by. From her posture, Anaïs could tell she had begrudgingly accepted that she wasn't in control of the vehicle, but this didn't prevent natural instincts from kicking in. Every now and then, normal human reactions took over and her hands sprang to the steering wheel in anticipation of something in their path. Her assistance was entirely unnecessary. The Morris Minor weaved through the traffic on the busy highway. Each time the car changed lanes, lateral forces sent Anaïs sliding across the back seat.

The little car was entertaining its occupants with its disc-jockey skills. After a period of surfing the frequencies, the car had found a cheerful tune to play. This was no mean feat as the majority of the AM radio band was filled with talk shows. The talking did not bother Anaïs. She thought the French language had its own form of musicality. She watched the librarian's head bob back and forth to the music and grinned.

From the moment they'd met, the librarian had grated on her nerves. She still did, but less so now. Anaïs had softened to her abrasive personality. She had tried not to let Immi's irritating behaviour bother her. She now saw the humour in it. Immi was funny. Their present predicament was not the librarian's fault. She didn't want to be there any more than the rest of them. They had just been thrown together. Whether she liked it or not, they were all unwilling passengers along for the ride.

Anaïs tried to stretch her legs. As a five-year-old there would have been more than enough room to lie flat across the back seat. In her eight-year-old body, she couldn't extend them full-length any more. She rolled onto her back and propped her feet up on the armrest affixed to the door. She stared up at the roof of the car and watched alternating shadows and flashes of light play across it. She listened to the hum of the tyres on the road. Occasionally they rumbled over a particularly rough section of bitumen, and strong vibrations would run through the chassis and seat and into her body. It was like getting massaged. It felt good.

Anaïs closed her eyes. She concentrated on her body.

She mentally assessed it and its dimensions. She had not yet had the chance to fully take stock of her transformation. It was a huge, unsettling change. *Was this sort of thing going to happen more often?* She wanted to look in a mirror properly and take the time to evaluate the new her. She wanted to look at her face. To scrutinise it.

She ran a hand over the length of her body from her knees, along her thighs, across her chest and up to her neck. Everything had stretched—not just her limbs, her skull too. She flexed her wrists and ankles. With her forefingers she stroked the features of her face. The baby plumpness had all but disappeared. She felt the sharp line of her temporal ridge, the hardness of her nose, cheekbones and chin.

'Are you ok, Anaïs?'

She opened her eyes and looked up at Nan. The shade was studying her intently.

'Yes, I'm fine,' said Anaïs. 'Just trying to come to terms with my new body.'

Nan ran her eyes along the length of the little witch's body and nodded. *'It must be strange.'*

Anaïs tried to read the shade's face but it was difficult without the sunglasses. She could only really see her eyes. She read concern in them. She thought about what Nan must be feeling. 'I'm pretty sure it's not as strange as what you're having to deal with.'

Nan's voice had a determined edge. *'I'm trying not to think about it.'*

The shade shuffled in her seat. Anaïs lifted her head and repositioned the coat under it.

'*One consolation is I don't have to deal with a stupid physical body any more. For you, change is ongoing. There will be many more to deal with. You still have a long way to go, Anaïs.*'

Anaïs nodded. 'Yes, that's what worries me.'

'*Don't worry too much. We will get through it together.*'

Anaïs smiled up at her. 'Thanks, that's good to know.'

Nan stroked her hair and parted the fringe on her forehead. '*Rest now, Anaïs.*'

The little witch closed her eyes and let the tension in her body go. She listened to the rhythm of the car's wheels on the road once more. The sound began to lull her to sleep.

The Morris Minor broke the tranquillity. Its speakers crackled loudly. It cranked the volume on the sound system up to full. Black Sabbath's 'War Pigs' blared out of the speakers. The engine whined and then practically screamed in unison with the music. The car shot forward.

The sudden acceleration drove Anaïs's head deep into Nan's lap. It pinned them both to the backrest of the seat. The witch gritted her teeth and with some difficulty pivoted her head. She looked across at the librarian. Immi's body was also pressed deep into her seat. Her neck arched, she strained against the gravitational forces brought on by the sudden increase in velocity. Her face had gone white, pure terror visible in her wide eyes.

IN PURSUIT

Anaïs struggled into a sitting position and craned her neck. She twisted in her seat, stuck her head over the top of it and looked out the rear window. A very large black car sat on their bumper. The vehicles were almost touching. It was so close half its bonnet was obscured by the rear of the Morris Minor.

The car bobbed up and down behind them as it rode the undulations of the highway's uneven surface. Its windscreen reflected sunlight, preventing Anaïs from seeing into the vehicle. She squinted but couldn't even make out the silhouette of a figure in the front seat. She hoped they shared her problem and couldn't see her staring back at them either. She sank down into her seat and turned to Nan.

'We have a problem,' she said.

'You don't say? It seems we have attracted some attention.' The caretaker looked over her shoulder at the car

behind them. *'Have you had this sort of problem before? Someone following you like this?'*

'Yes,' said Anaïs grimly. 'After I lost you, we were chased by a man and a dog.'

The shade looked down at Anaïs and then stared at the seat in front of her. *'The Inquisitor,'* she said.

Anaïs raised an eyebrow. 'Is that what he's called? Sounds pretty ominous.'

'Yes, that's what the Organisation call him. I don't think they know his real name.'

'I don't think knowing his real name would make much difference. Except if it was something weird. You know? Like Cuthbert or Cecil or Ernest.'

The librarian sniped loudly from the front seat. 'What are you going on about?' She fiddled with the volume knob on the radio. To her surprise the Morris Minor obliged and reduced the noise.

'I don't know,' said Anaïs. 'I guess I'm a little on edge. I tend to say the strangest things when I'm under pressure. What's going on in front?'

The librarian took a deep breath and expelled it. 'We are going really fast. I thought that was obvious. And you say the strangest things when you're *not* under pressure as well.'

Anaïs sneered at her. 'Thanks. I got the whole speed thing. I was just wondering if the car was telling you anything else.'

The librarian's eyes flicked from the rear-vision mirror to the speedometer. 'Only how fast we're going. And I wish it didn't have to play heavy metal while it's doing it.'

'I kind of like it. Maybe it's trying to say something with the song?'

The librarian screwed up her face. 'I'm afraid all I hear is some guy screaming and a bunch of very loud guitars.'

'It's an anti-war song. That's all I know. Ozzie did say something about witches at the start, though.'

'Ozzie? Who's Ozzie?'

'Ozzie Osbourne. Don't you know anything?'

The librarian frowned. 'Of course I do. Isn't he that weird British guy that used to be on TV? The one with the crabby wife and stuck-up kids? He seemed to be perpetually stoned.' She grinned to herself. 'Not a surprise really, considering who he has to live with.'

'Yeah.' Anaïs nodded and then shook her head in disbelief. 'That guy from TV.' She decided not to waste any more time trying to explain the singer's previous claim to fame to the librarian.

'Where has she been living? Under a rock?'

'Beats me,' said Anaïs smirking. 'She certainly hasn't been listening to any.'

Anaïs heard Nan chuckling in her head. It made her smile. Then the smile dissipated. This was no laughing matter. Anaïs turned in her seat again and looked over the top of the backrest. The car was still there.

'What's it doing?'

'It's just hanging there.' Anaïs watched the vehicle bob around behind them, hanging on to their rear as if glued to it. The Morris Minor weaved its way through a thick clump of vehicles. It slowed to negotiate overtaking a particularly large truck. Anaïs felt her eardrums pop with the change in pressure as they neared it. The Morris Minor found a gap in traffic and skirted around the truck. The black car followed its every move, constantly maintaining its hold on the bumper of the little car. Once they had passed the truck the Morris Minor accelerated, its little engine roaring so loud it even drowned out the music.

They were now out of heavy traffic and the road opened up before them. Anaïs looked around. They were very exposed. There were no more trees lining the highway, only open fields. She arched her neck and looked at the sky above through the rear window. It too was clear. She squirmed uncomfortably in her seat. She felt more vulnerable than ever.

'What's up?' asked Nan.

'I have the feeling we're being watched and can't shake the idea that whatever it is could come from anywhere.'

The caretaker flicked her head towards the vehicle. *'You mean watched by someone other than the car?'*

Anaïs turned in her seat and looked at the car again. The sun had gone behind a cloud and now she could see into the vehicle. She saw the headrests of the front seats. There were no heads resting on them. The vehicle was empty. The only movement inside it was its steering wheel twitching from right to left and back again. She shuddered.

Suddenly the black car slowed. It peeled off into the other lane. She watched it recede behind them. It veered off the highway and up an exit ramp. The ramp curved up onto a bridge spanning the highway. The car stopped when it reached the middle of the bridge. It became a speck in the distance and then disappeared altogether as they rounded a bend in the road. Anaïs breathed out slowly through pursed lips.

'It's gone,' she said.

The librarian yelled to make herself heard above the din in the cabin.

'Good!'

The Morris Minor made no change in its trajectory and maintained its high speed, barrelling down the highway. Anaïs was left to wonder what had been following them. Not only that, she still didn't know where they were going. She wished her promptuary would come back online. She looked down at it lying on the seat beside her. The only sign of life was the star on the cover, slowly pulsing as if it was in sleep mode, almost like an ordinary electronic device.

SPAIN

The roads on the outskirts of Barcelona were a spaghetti of overpasses, underpasses, bridges, tunnels and ring routes. The Morris Minor zigzagged its way through the late-afternoon traffic, unperturbed by the meandering roads. Anaïs was thankful the Morris Minor was in control. None of them would have had any idea how to find their way through the city streets—not that they knew what their destination was anyway. Looking out her window as they descended through the suburbs, she saw they were heading towards the taller buildings at the centre of the city. Beyond them she could see the blue glint of the Mediterranean. She wondered what awaited them.

They had made their journey swiftly. She wasn't certain how far they had travelled but it seemed to have been a great distance. They had only made one stop at a fuelling station. Not to provide the car with any nourishment; the librarian had needed sustenance. The rumbling of her stomach had become so acute it had threatened to drown out the noise of the engine.

Surprisingly the Morris Minor was in need of nothing. Its fuel gauge had not moved for the entire trip. During their stop Anaïs had taken a careful look at it. The hand on the dial was nestled hard up against the top position. It was slightly bent as if trying to force its way beyond the full position. Whatever magical fumes the car ran on must have been extremely powerful.

The Morris Minor had sat idling impatiently in the parking lot whilst the librarian went to get some food. She had barely received her order when it had begun tooting its horn, insisting she return. Clearly the car was on a mission to get them to their destination as quickly as possible. The librarian had come running back and demanded to know what all the noise was about. Anaïs had shrugged and explained that the car was in charge and not her. This had set off another altercation between them. The car had attempted to silence them by revving its engine. When this proved fruitless it had engaged its gear and started to trundle to the exit of the parking lot and back to the highway. Apparently the Morris Minor was not only on a tight schedule but also had an aversion to bickering.

The librarian had been forced to run after the vehicle. Clacking wonkily along on her high heels, with a mountain of food in her arms, she had caught up with the car as it started to accelerate. She had thrown herself through the open door into the front seat. The librarian had yelled and cursed at the vehicle. It had slammed the driver's door shut, narrowly avoiding slicing off her leg which had been hanging out of the car. She pulled in the trailing limb just in time. The door shut on the shoulder of her coat. The Morris Minor engaged the locks and refused to open its door. Immi had been forced to sit with one ear pressed to the driver's side window. She had smouldered in silence for the remainder of the journey.

Anaïs began to take a shine to the car. It seemed to be the only thing that could successfully quell the librarian's insipid comments. She knew, however, that the vehicle would not take sides. She also needed to be wary of what she said to it. Nevertheless, she liked its style.

The Morris Minor left the arterial roads and entered the streets of Barcelona proper. It wound its way through small streets and then onto long, dead-straight boulevards. Anaïs watched the blocks of buildings flash by. They gradually changed from an austere style to something more ornate. The architecture seemed to be taking them back in time. It was then she saw the strangest thing sticking out above the buildings. It was enormous. A set of church spires unlike any she had seen before. Almost like trees in a small forest, they towered above their surroundings. They were honeycombed and, rather than topped with crosses, they were decorated with what looked like flowers. There was something entirely organic about the structure.

Anaïs's jaw dropped. The librarian saw it as well, and the snarl which had been fixed on her face for most of the trip was replaced with a look of astonishment. The Morris Minor slowed and rounded a final corner, revealing the entire building before them. It parked across the road from what appeared to be the main entrance, although this was difficult to ascertain. Sections of it were lit up and, when the late afternoon sun dipped behind a cloud and more artificial light appeared, the church seemed to be in a state of transformation.

Anaïs climbed out of the car and looked up at the huge building before her. 'What kind of magic is this?'

'*Very human magic,*' said the nanny, now standing beside the little witch. '*I've seen this before, many years ago, but then it was so different. There was not so much of it. They have been busy. Anaïs, this is one of the wonders of the real world. This is La Sagrada Familia.*'

THE ARCHITECT

'*Permís! Excuse me. You're in my way.*'

The man behind Anaïs sat on the fence with a writing block on his lap. He waved her to move. His brow was furrowed. He looked irritated, even through his camouflage.

He persisted, not looking directly at her but over her shoulder. He waved his hand in the air. '*I can't see.*'

Anaïs stepped to one side. 'Oh, I'm sorry.'

The shade did not look at her but from his sketch pad to the enormous building in front of him. He cocked his head to one side and compared the images. His eyes flicked from pad to building and back again.

Anaïs was irritated herself. The guy was rude. 'I said I'm sorry,' she repeated forcefully.

'*Sí, sí, gràcies.*' He brushed her off and buried his head in his work.

She wondered what he would have done if a natural had stood in his line of sight. He would not be able to tell one of them to move. Here was another shade who had picked her out of the crowd. He knew she was a witch. This was becoming all too commonplace. It bothered her and she felt exposed. She looked around to see if anyone else was looking at them. Nobody was.

They were across the road and far enough down the street not to be caught in the crowd of tourists. Packs of them milled around in front of the basilica. Couples on their honeymoons and families with teenage children took turns taking snapshots of one another. Anaïs's attention was drawn to a particularly handsome teenage boy. He was to die for. Spanish boys were dreamy. There was something about their dark looks that did it for her. He was putting on an act of being overly-cool. She smiled at him and raised her eyebrows. He saw the look and it threw him. He blushed and then looked confused, registering her apparent age. He regained his composure and turned his back on her.

Anaïs turned red, realising her place. Her teenage hormones were going haywire and it took all her concentration to get a handle on them. She had to find a way to curb her desires. She had to make an effort to act her physical age or it would get her in trouble.

She shook her head to clear her thoughts and turned back to the shade. That was where her focus should be. The man was balanced precariously on the thin top rung of the metal fence. He almost floated there, his feet not touching the ground. He rocked backwards and forwards as he sketched. She watched him work.

His hand glided effortlessly over the page. Black ink began to fill the empty white slate. At first he moved slowly and then he sped up. He worked furiously on his artwork, pausing every now and then to assess the building in front of him before diving back into his drawing. His hand eventually began moving so fast she could barely see it. The image on the page miraculously appeared by itself. It was beautiful and the detail was incredible.

This is no ordinary street artist, thought Anaïs.

He spat and cursed to himself. *'Renoi! They have it wrong again. Why can't they just stick to the plans?'*

He ripped the page out of the pad and scrunched it up into a ball. Anaïs was mystified. How was it he could influence a physical object? He threw the ball of paper with all his might and nearly lost his balance, almost toppling backwards off the fence. The paper ball flew in a long arc towards the crowd of tourists across the street. Before it hit one of them it vanished.

So the writing materials were not real. Or, at least, they were not part of his camouflage. They were part of what lay beneath. Perhaps her powers of perception were increasing. Could it be that as she grew, she would start to see less and less of a shade's camouflage?

This could present a problem. If she could no longer see what the normal world saw, how would she know how to react to people? With her previous shade experience, she had been able to explain to the shade's daughter that what she saw before her was not really her father. She had been able to pass him off as just some old man. If this changed, if she didn't know what a shade looked like in disguise, how would she know what to say?

She turned her attention back to the shade in hand.

He had jumped down from the fence and was stuffing his sketchbook into his jacket. He went to leave and she moved to stop him.

'Excuse me, sir?'

He stopped and looked at her. *'Sí? Can I help you?'*

'Maybe.' She paused to consider him. He looked like a beggar. His suit was shabby and white beard unkempt. She wondered if she was seeing a disguise at all. The way his eyes twinkled seemed far too real. Perhaps this was the real him.

'Just a moment please,' she said.

She fumbled around in her beret and found what she was looking for. She pulled out her sunglasses and slipped them on. She was startled to see no discernible change in his appearance.

'Do you know who you are?' she enquired.

He puffed out his chest and knotted his brow as if insulted. *'Of course! Why should I not know that?'*

Anaïs was not sure what he really knew and said gently, 'You do know you're dead?'

'Sí, sí.' He chewed on his bottom lip, played with his beard and nodded his head gravely. *'I know. It is a curse but it is, how you say it, the way things are?'* He brightened and smiled. *'It is good. I am happy. I can continue my work. I take it as a blessing.'*

'But who are you?'

He held out his hand. *'Antoni, Antoni Gaudí. And your name is?'*

She stiffened herself against the chill and shook his hand. 'Anaïs, my name is Anaïs.'

He released his grip and spread his arms wide. *'Preciós! Beautiful! You have a beautiful name.'*

Anaïs turned a shade of red again. 'Thank you.'

'This is my beauty.' He spun and swung his arm towards the basilica. *'One day she will be finished. And then people will see how beautiful she truly is.'*

Anaïs looked up at the forest of spires towering above them. The building was already spectacular, even in its unfinished state.

'This is why I am here. This is more important than life or death. Because of her I can never forget. She is with me every day. She reminds me who I am. She reminds me why I am here.'

'Then you have something very special,' said Anaïs. 'Not everyone is as lucky as you.'

He grabbed the witch passionately by the shoulders. He flashed his bright blue eyes at her. She fought the urge to shiver.

'I will stay with her until she is finished,' he said with determination. *'I will complete her, no matter how long it takes.'*

He released his hold on the little witch and shook his fist at the basilica. *'Now! If only those* gilipolles *can get it right!'*

A movement across the street caught Anaïs's eye. It was the oddest thing she had ever seen. Even stranger than the bombastic La Sagrada Familia itself.

A TICKING CLOCK

How long do we have? The living definitely have a limited shelf life, but what about shades? And what about witches, for that matter?

Witches can live for centuries, but at some point their earthly shells also perish. Then, what do they become? Do they also enter the shade world? If they do, how long do they spend on that plane of existence? Do they also have an exclusive pass there? Are they exempt from all the usual shade idiosyncrasies?

I'm sorry I brought this up. I'm afraid I don't have all the answers. At the very beginning I warned you about this. I am no witch and, honestly, I'm not sure witches even know what happens to them in the hereafter. Nobody really knows. One thing is certain—somewhere in the cosmos, there is a clock ticking, and it ticks for all of us.

I don't want to depress you but those are the facts of life. Or perhaps life is the wrong word. Shall we just call it: existence. We don't want to exclude any entities from this discussion.

However, delving into and considering the option of immortality presents problems. It is a major conundrum. Thinking about it too much will only give you a headache. There are just too many permutations. Our cerebrums have enough to do as it is.

The brain is a powerful organ but at some stage it will exhaust itself and self-destruct. It has a finite existence. Whether you live forever, or die forever for that matter, at some point it will be enough. Your noggin will have absorbed all it can possibly take and drown in information overload.

Aside from the possibility of immortality, is there really a purpose to gaining knowledge? The general tendency for the human race is to want to know it all. Their appetite for knowledge is insatiable. But there has to be a limit. Eventually you will have learnt everything of interest and done all there is to do. Either you will become bored or suffocate under the massive weight of your own knowledge. That is, unless you have another reason for sticking around.

Maybe you don't have a thirst for knowledge. Maybe you have learned enough. Perhaps you are satisfied with what you already have. Perhaps you want to do something useful with that knowledge.

What we had here on the streets of Barcelona was an oddity. A shade who *wanted* to be a shade. He was quite content with his existence. At least this one had something useful to do. He had purpose.

But the mere idea of enjoying your death, how

weird is that? It's positively morbid. Who in their right mind would find hanging between here and there appealing? Clearly Mr Gaudi had other things on his mind. He wasn't concerned with his own existence. He had another obsession. He had found his gift and was exercising it. There is nothing wrong with that. His problem had been solved. He knew what his one true purpose was.

This meant Anaïs wasn't required. She didn't need to offer any assistance. Mr Gaudi was doing fine on his own. He was in his element. He was doing something useful. Or, at least, he was under the impression that what he was doing was valuable. Unfortunately, nobody knew he was still around and working on his creation. This was not a problem in itself.

Construction was continuing on his epos. His life's work, his magnum opus, was being built. The architects and engineers working on the basilica had his original plans and sketches. They were painstakingly adhering to his vision. He was not aware of this, but that was not important. He could amuse himself with an afterlife of doodling and not disturb anyone.

Eventually the building would be completed and then he would find peace, or perhaps not. I cannot predict the future and nor can witches. At any rate, his core ideas would find a physical form. There should be some kind of satisfaction in that fact.

Men like Mr Gaudi are very rarely satisfied. His perfectionism knew no end—no bounds. He would continue until the end of time with his preoccupation. With respect to perfectionism, time is immaterial. It is likely Mr Gaudi would remain standing across the street from his basilica for eternity. Perhaps that is immortality, following a joyful preoccupation until the end of time. Happiness to the power of infinity.

If he had no purpose it would be different. Without a purpose he could possibly be dangerous. His obsession could drive him to influence the physical world. Thankfully he was unaware of this and was content to exercise his passion with his creation.

This probably goes some way to explaining why entities such as the Inquisitor existed in the first place. Somebody needs to keep it all in check. If at least one of these alternative thinkers existed, there would have to be more. If word spread that being a shade was good there could be problems. If the planet was filled with shades who all decided they liked their lot, eventually there would be no room for the living.

DEAD SEXY

The shade had an aura around it stronger than any other Anaïs had ever experienced. If it had been alive it probably would have stopped traffic. Even in death it wasn't going unnoticed. It caught the eye of the naturals around it, although they self-consciously averted their eyes as it walked by. It exuded something very special.

Anaïs felt something deep. She was moved emotionally. It was the strangest thing. She watched the shade walk along the other side of the street. It had emerged out of the crowd gathered in front of the basilica. She could have sworn the naturals had parted to let it through. Its hips swayed hypnotically. It oozed sex. Anaïs felt her heart flutter. She swooned. There was a moment of enchantment, of desire, almost like love at first sight, and then it was gone. It took her breath away. She pulled herself together.

On the surface, physically, there was something extremely peculiar about the shade. Foremost was its appearance. Its camouflage was amazing. It was smartly dressed in a pinstriped business suit. Neat, crisp creases ran along the sleeves and down the front of the trousers. The thinnest of ties fitted snugly in a chokehold around its neck. Everything about it was immaculate. It appeared to have spent hours in front of the mirror perfecting its look.

Its hair was slicked back and adhered to its skull, encasing it in a tight-fitting helmet. A layer of powdered make-up created a gleaming, white porcelain sheen on its face. Jet-black eyebrows were finely pencilled across its forehead, terminating in sharp points on its temples. Bright, red lipstick sliced across its mouth, making their lips stand out and almost spring off its face. It wore the highest heels Anaïs had ever seen but carried itself as if floating on air. Most bewildering of all, it had a refined and neatly trimmed beard.

The librarian's jaw dropped. 'Wow!' she exclaimed.

Anaïs grinned up at her. 'You see it too?'

The librarian nodded slowly, not taking her eyes off the odd apparition across the street.

Anaïs moved in close to her and gave her a nudge. 'It's a shade.'

'Oh?' The librarian studied the shade. 'Is it male or female?'

Anaïs ran her eyes up and down the shade. 'That's debatable. It looks like a bit of both. I'm not sure what lies underneath the disguise, but on the outside it's the best-dressed drag queen I've ever seen. Or should that be drag king?'

Immi raised an eyebrow and cocked her head to one side. 'What do you want to do?'

'Follow it,' said Anaïs.

She threw one last look at the little architect. He had returned to his perch on the fence and was now kneading a piece of clay between his fingers. He appeared to be sculpting an animal of some description. He worked fast. She watched the clay in his hands begin to form a contorted mix between a bird and an elephant. He was so engrossed in his creation, he failed to acknowledge the little witch, even when she waved a hand in front of his eyes. Anaïs left him to his preoccupation. He was harmless. The spectre, or rather spectacle, across the road was another thing altogether.

The shade had moved further down the street. Without taking her eyes off it, Anaïs ran to catch up. Running ungainly on her high heels, the librarian struggled to keep up. Anaïs stayed on her side of the street and shadowed the apparition until it stopped in front of a huge plate-glass shop window.

The shade reached into its suit pocket and produced a little square, gold-plated tin and a matching gold cylinder. The cylinder was no longer than its thumb. The shade turned its back to the window. It removed the cap from the cylinder and screwed its base. A bright-red tube of lipstick emerged. It flipped open the tin. It was a compact with a mirror inserted into the lid. Anaïs saw the mirror glint in the sun. As the shade brought the compact up to its face, the reflected sunlight flashed across the facade of the building.

The shade looked over its shoulder at the window

behind it. It lined itself up so that it could see its own reflection in the compact's mirror. Anaïs watched it pull its lips taut across its face and meticulously apply the lipstick. Satisfied with its appearance, it dropped the lipstick in a suit pocket. It pulled an embroidered handkerchief out of its trousers. The shade peered into the compact and patted its lips.

The librarian pulled up next to Anaïs, puffing.

The little witch frowned. 'This is not good.'

'What?' The librarian tried to catch her breath.

'The shade, it's flaunting itself.' Anaïs turned and assessed the librarian. She frowned. 'You're not very fit, are you?'

The librarian leaned forward, resting her hands on her knees. 'Of course I am,' Immi panted. 'You try running in these things.' She nodded at her stilettos.

'No thanks,' said Anaïs.

'What are you worried about anyway?' The librarian straightened and tossed her head dismissively at the shade across the street. 'Perhaps the best disguise is one where you don't hide. Nobody else seems to be worried about it.' She cracked her back and looked down the street. 'In fact, I think, if anything, it's driving people away rather than attracting them.'

Anaïs shook her head. 'No, I think this is going too far.'

'You think?' The librarian examined her own manicured fingernails and scrutinised the shade. 'It looks fantastic. I, for one, am impressed.'

'You would be. Are you going to take notes?'

'Maybe,' said the librarian with a hint of sarcasm.

Nan stepped into the line of sight of the two women. The librarian scowled at her for blocking her view and looked over her shoulder at the shade across the road.

The caretaker folded her arms and eyeballed them. *'Can the two of you stop?'*

Anaïs was irritated and also tried to look past Nan. 'What do you mean?'

'Stop arguing,' said the shade.

'Ok, then, I will do that,' said Immi, not hearing the shade.

'Do what?' enquired Anaïs perplexed.

'Take notes.'

Anaïs shook her head. 'No, Nan just told us to stop fighting.' She turned her attention to her caretaker. 'We're not arguing, Nan.'

The librarian pulled a face and rolled her eyes. 'I'm not taking orders from a shade.'

Anaïs sighed. 'Whatever! Listen, I'm curious to know who it really is. Aren't you?' She rummaged in her beret and pulled out her sunglasses. 'Let's have a look.'

Anaïs polished the lenses using the corner of her coat. She hooked the sunglasses over her ears. The world turned a reassuring shade of purple. She focussed on the shade. Her eyes widened. 'Wow!'

'What is it?' exclaimed the librarian.

Nan turned to look at the shade. *'Yes, what? Who is it?'*

Anaïs was beside herself. 'Wow!' she said again.

The librarian puffed her cheeks. 'Enough already with the wows. Who is it?'

Anaïs stared open-mouthed at the shade. She failed

to hear the other women. She was dumbfounded. 'You won't believe who it is.'

Nan looked at Anaïs. *'We won't have the opportunity to believe anything unless you tell us.'* The caretaker became infuriated. *'Tell us!'*

Anaïs was preoccupied with her own thoughts. She doubted her first impression. She lifted the sunglasses and peered out under them. She repositioned them on the bridge of her nose. She tilted her head and knotted her brow.

'No, maybe not,' she said with uncertainty. 'I'm not sure.'

She took the glasses off, dropped them in her beret and stepped around Nan. 'Wait here. I need to get a closer look.'

THE LOOKING GLASS

Mirrors reveal all. Even the things we don't particularly want to see. They expose us to ourselves.

In the case of shades, mirrors reveal their true selves. Mirrors enable them to see beneath their camouflage. In general, this is the only way a shade perceives itself. As a shade it is very difficult to see your own disguise. Naturally, you do see elements of your camouflage if you look down at your body. But if you look at your reflection you will only see what lies beneath. The only way to see your camouflage as a shade is in a reflection of a reflection.

If you hold something up to a mirror you will see it in reverse. This is particularly obvious when you hold a piece of text up to a mirror. It is disguised. Not only is it in reverse, it is inverted. If you use a second mirror the text will be reversed once more. The original will become apparent. It will be revealed as it truly is. It's magic.

Most shades are unaware of this trick. Most of them assume the rest of the world is able to see the real them. This is not surprising, as it is the way they see themselves. On rare occasions shades have come to understand the nature of their predicament. However, without outside help very few crack the secrets hidden behind a mirror.

Naturals have always had a soft spot for preening themselves in front of reflective surfaces. A high quality mirror was very difficult to come by in ancient times and the modern mirror was not advanced until the Venetians set their minds to it. It's not really surprising they were the ones to advance this technology, considering how self-absorbed and fashion-conscious they were. Also, they had the added advantage of being experts in glass blowing.

Before the Venetians founded a thriving industry in mirror making, a pool of water was your best option. Stones were polished for portability. Later, with the development of alloys, sheets of metal were used. However, the reflections were rarely flattering, or flat. It is a complicated process to achieve a perfectly uniform surface. In order to see a reflection, you need a smooth surface much more than something that is a particularly good reflector. Also, a metal alloy such as copper or bronze produces a tinted reflection. Perfectly fine if you prefer to see yourself with a permanent suntan. However, it requires a serious amount of work to keep such a surface clean and shiny.

The worldwide obsession with perfecting something to satisfy people's egos continued. Searching for the ideal mirror took millennia. This did have the advantage of concealing the dead from the living. There are now considerably more opportunities to see them uncovered. That is, if you know where to look. Fortunately, most naturals are too busy looking at their own reflections and not those of others.

Developments in glass-making provided a better, although complex, solution to maintaining a polished reflective surface. Glass makes an excellent coating for a sheet of metal. Even with its advent, the flatness of a mirror could not be perfected. Blowing glass usually produces something that is concave, creating a distorted reflection. In the end, alchemy played a decisive role.

The global obsession with vanity got dirty. Where money is involved this invariably occurs. The first mirrors were very valuable objects and rumours abound that someone even offered an entire country estate for one. Supposedly they thought it was a good deal. This demand led to the final stage in mirror development.

Witches got involved in the spread of this much-sought-after technology. One of them broke the cardinal rule of not influencing the real world. Financial reward was not the catalyst; looking good was. Vanity is an affliction not confined to naturals. An especially vain witch, using her alchemist connections, encouraged industrial espionage. Strategically dropped hints were placed in open ears, and the technique of adhering a perfect reflective surface to a glass coating presented the Venetians with a golden opportunity to cash in. The modern mirror achieved near perfection.

In order for them to work properly, mirrors depend

on reflecting a high quantity of light. Without light there is no reflection. So how do shades see themselves? They are shadows, after all. A light burns within all of us. Dead or alive this inner source of power shines through. I cannot tell you why this is or how it exists. Just take my word for it. Religious beliefs and other organisations have given it a name. Witches also have a name for it. They call it the source. You know you have it. You can feel it. As long as anybody exists on any plane, supernatural or natural, it is there. It is where we draw our vitality from. The source is an energy so powerful it will always shine through.

Anaïs was about to meet someone who had discovered the key to manipulating reflection. This shade was special. It was incredibly vain. This preoccupation was so strong it had helped it harness and take control of death—something quite odd, really. Its drive for perfection, for outer looks, had led it to the discovery of the simple but complex nature of mirrors. All this narcissism came from a lifetime spent in front of one of them. It had a deep affinity with the reflected image. It had found a way to see not only itself but also the camouflage that covered it. It had altered its own disguise.

This shade was an abnormality, an anomaly.

THE MISFIT

The little witch looked up at the shade and gave it a nudge. 'Do you always do this?'

The shade looked down at her incredulously. *'Excuse me, child, did you say something?'*

Anaïs smiled to herself. It was a woman's voice echoing in her head. 'Yes, I did. I said, "Do you always do this?"'

'Do what?'

'Flaunt yourself. You know, parade around dressed like this.'

The shade pointed at its chest. *'You mean like this?'*

Anaïs nodded.

The shade slouched and put a hand on its hip. *'There's nothing wrong with this.'* It looked over its shoulder, lifted a foot and flexed its ankle. It examined its footwear. *'Give a girl the right shoes and she can conquer the world.'*

The librarian, slightly out of breath, pulled up beside Anaïs. 'Can you please not take off like that?' She studied the shade's face, ran her eyes over the rest of its body and frowned. 'What did it say?'

Anaïs turned to Immi. '*She* said something about a woman's shoes conquering the world.'

The librarian grinned. 'Oh! I like this one already.'

Anaïs rolled her eyes. 'You would!'

'Who is it, by the way?'

'I'm not sure yet. I'm still checking.'

'*So, you're a witch then?*'

Anaïs took a step back in surprise. 'Yes, how did you know?'

'*For a start you can hear me. You're not the first one I've met.*'

'Really?'

'*Most of them are not as forward as you, but yes, I've met a few.*'

'Is that so?'

The shade nodded. '*Just like you, they're always warning me not to be so blatant about my appearance. They tend to worry I'll expose myself. I usually tell them to leave me alone.*' She held the compact up to her face and examined her features. '*It's not that I don't appreciate their concern, but I prefer to do my own thing. It is better to be absolutely ridiculous than absolutely boring. I like what I do. I do what I like.*'

'You mean you like it this way, being a shade and all?'

'*Of course! What's not to like? Living was scary. Death is easy.*' She grabbed Anaïs by the forearm. Her grip was a little too firm. A cold spike ran the length of the witch's arm. It shot all the way up to her shoulder and the entire limb went numb. The shade pulled her across to a nearby advertising pillar. It was decorated with shards of broken mirror. They were glued onto the masonry, completely covering it like a mirror ball. *'Look! Do you recognise me?'*

Anaïs squinted at the reflection in the collection of little mirrors. The image of the shade without its camouflage was splintered but still discernible. She saw exactly what she had seen from across the road. A woman in her mid thirties, crowned with a shock of platinum blonde hair. She wore a strapless, sleek, ankle-length dress which clung to her body and left very little to the imagination. Anaïs was delighted with the colour: a brilliant tone of electric purple. The shade had a slender waist and an extreme hour-glass figure. She pouted at Anaïs. The witch could now clearly see her face, which had been obscured before.

Her eyes lit up and a grin split her face. 'I knew it. It is you. Marilyn? Marilyn Monroe?'

The librarian's eyes widened in disbelief. 'What?'

The shade swelled her generous breast and proudly proclaimed, *'Indeed, the one and only!'*

Anaïs began to shake uncontrollably. The shade's icy grip had spread beyond her arm and through the rest of her body. It hurt and she grimaced. She clamped her jaw shut to stop her teeth chattering and murmured, 'Could you please let go of my arm?'

Marilyn released her grip. *'Oh, I'm sorry. Of course.'* She kneaded her hands as if trying to warm them.

Anaïs rubbed her shoulder and shook her arm in an effort to get the blood flowing again. She flexed her fingers and squeezed the tips together. The feeling began to return.

'But …' stammered the librarian.

Anaïs ignored her. 'It's a pleasure to meet you,' she said.

'Oh, the pleasure is all mine,' said Marilyn.

Anaïs went to shake her hand but thought better of it. Her arm had only just returned to a normal temperature. 'Why do you take such risks with your appearance? Don't you know there are unfriendly forces out there looking for people like you?'

'Yes, I know. I've seen them. They are pretty easy to spot. But they don't bother me. Well, at least, I don't let them bother me.'

'Anaïs? We have to go.' This time the voice in her head was Nan's.

'Not right now, Nan,' said Anaïs with an edge of irritation. 'I'm talking.' She turned away from the mirrors which now also held Nan's image. She looked at the camouflaged Marilyn. It was a very good disguise, albeit a bit strange. 'Now I'm curious. How do you get away from them?'

'Easy. I'm a chameleon. I've had more than a lifetime of experience playing around with my appearance. If I want to, I am very good at hiding. Anyway, they always give themselves away.'

'How?'

'They're never alone. There is always some kind of strange beast hanging around with them.' Marilyn lifted her head and nodded with her chin at something behind Anaïs. *'Just like that one over there.'*

CONFRONTATION

Asly smile contorted his face. *This was too easy.* The Inquisitor let his hand drop and ran his knuckles over the dog's hard head. He pulled the cigar out of his mouth. Tilting back his head, he shot a jet of blue smoke into the air.

He weighed the situation. This time it was different. They were in a group. A big target. They had no transport. Even if they separated and went in opposite directions, he would still catch one of them. One shade was better than none at all.

The girl had aged. It had taken him by surprise. Her face was the same. A little more elongated and thinner, but it was definitely her. Before he left, they had said she was special and to be prepared for the extraordinary. A pity they could tell him no more. At least he now knew one thing. She was not a natural, nor was she a shade. He could discount her. He was not there for her. *Don't get distracted again. She is only bait.*

Just as before, the way she had been

communicating with them had given them away. He ran his eyes over the group. The cross-dresser, or whatever it was, and the old woman. They appeared apathetic and lethargic to him. They had to be shades. He was not sure about the other one, the one wearing a fluffy coat. She certainly dressed a lot like the bearded one, but she was not a shade. She was also strangely familiar. Had he seen her before? No matter. Chances were she was a natural. More animated than the others, she did not have the vacant stare of a shade. She was alive and kicking. He could forget about her. Whoever she was, it was irrelevant. She was not a target.

He drew deeply on the cigar and exhaled, letting the smoke pour out through his nostrils. The rather robust shade, the thick set woman, would not be able to move fast. The bearded one would be hampered by those incredibly high heels. *Excellent!*

He smirked again. He was in control. It was a good feeling. He studied the girl and had a passing moment of sympathy for her. She was very young. He was not entirely comfortable with the fact he was dealing with a child. The shades did not matter, for they had squandered their chance at life and their time was over. A child still had something to live for, even if that child was not entirely natural. Not that he had been tasked with getting rid of her. What happened to her was not strictly his concern, although deep down it troubled him. Whenever possible, he was tasked with protecting the innocent.

Stop thinking like that. Do your job, he urged himself.

He shook his head to clear it, furrowed his brow and focussed on the group across the street.

Right, let's get down to it then!

He twisted the dog's chain tighter around his palm. He took a last long pull on the cigar, dropped the butt at his feet and ground it into the pavement. This time he would not wait for them to make the first move. He had the advantage of surprise. He checked for traffic and stepped out onto the road.

Anaïs looked around frantically. How had he got here? She thought he was gone forever. She needed a distraction, anything, something to slow him down. A gust of wind whipped up a piece of paper and blew it across the street. It hit the Inquisitor in the leg and flapped around his boot. He stooped to pull it off. Then the thought struck her. She had something. She had recently played with it in Amsterdam. The weather there was perfect for it. There was always a breeze whipping across the flat plains in the Netherlands. She reached deep into her beret and pulled out a child's plastic windmill.

Why hadn't she thought of it before?

She pulled the beret down snuggly around her ears. She spread her legs, widening her stance. She leant forward slightly and set her weight against the windmill and gripped it with both hands. She blew softly through the vanes.

The windmill slowly began to turn. She blew again

and it sped up. It began making a whirring noise. The blades of the toy became a solid circle and she could no longer make out the individual vanes. Little sparks of light started to flicker on the circumference until there was a completely stable ring of light.

She turned her attention to the man and his dog crossing the road towards them. She adjusted her stance and directed the toy at them. The first indication of its effect was when the dog's fringe parted on its snout. The fur flapped back up over its broad skull and exposed its bright red eyes. She ignored them and focussed on the toy in her hands. She willed the windmill on. The whirring sound amplified as its velocity increased. It emitted an almost hypnotic drone. A halo of light grew around it.

Loose rubbish lying on the road between her and the Inquisitor fluttered. Flapping first at the edges, it soon became airborne. A plastic bag flew at the Inquisitor and wrapped itself around his face. He tore it off and didn't break stride. More rubbish levitated into the air. Caught in the unseen wind it flew towards the Inquisitor. Each piece that struck him, he wrenched from his body and discarded, until an entire movie poster extracted itself from a nearby fence and soared across the street. It hit him, covering him from head to foot, stopping him in his tracks. The edges of the poster shredded and wrapped around his legs, torso and head. He fought vainly to rip it off but the paper was too thick.

More and more discarded wrappers, paper bags, bits of plastic and other packaging added to the coating around his body. Eventually the Inquisitor was completely wrapped in refuse. He continued the fight to free himself, thrashing his arms until they too were pinned to his body. The heavy bulk of trash forced him backwards. He took one step and lost his balance, his legs tangled in a mass of rubbish. He fell.

He slid along the ground away from her, packaged like a colourful Christmas present, dragging the dog with him. It too struggled, its claws digging deep into the asphalt. It could not compete with the invisible wind and the added weight of the Inquisitor. The wrappers drove them back to where they had first stood and then beyond, towards a high, metal fence surrounding the basilica's building site.

A movement halfway up the closest steeple caught her eye. A figure, dressed entirely in black, in a long coat and sporting a fedora, stood on an exposed staircase. It held onto a railing and leaned out of the tower. It watched the scene play out below. Its attention was focussed solely on the Inquisitor. Above the church a thick, dark cloud was forming. Its blackness dominated the sky. Anaïs heard the rumble of thunder. Then something else distracted her. A hand gripped her shoulder.

She tried to shrug it off but it held her firm. She took one hand off the windmill. It was more difficult to control and wobbled erratically in her hand. It took almost all of her willpower to keep it aimed at the Inquisitor. With her free hand she tried to pry the fingers off her shoulder. She dared not look away from her target and what she was doing for fear the magic would falter. She fought to maintain her concentration.

The hand pulled her backwards, guiding her around a corner and into the neighbouring side street. The last she saw of the Inquisitor, he and his dog were a great ball of paper plastered against the metal fence.

The hand spun her around. She looked at the face of its owner. Her initial irritation melted and turned to joy. A broad smile lit up her own face. It was one face she was more than pleased to see.

LA FARMÀCIA

'Wow! You have a great setup here,' said Anaïs.

'It's ok, I suppose,' muttered the Apothecary. 'But I miss my sound system.'

'Why don't you get a new one?'

'I will, once I can work out how to ask for one in Spanish.' He scratched his head. 'I only just got here.'

'Why did they transfer you?'

'They thought it would be good for me. A change of climate, I guess. Nice weather and all that. I couldn't care less. I hate the sun.'

Anaïs grinned at him. 'Yeah, a lot of good that does you now. It's the middle of winter. I'm not sure you'll get much sun right now.'

'Good, I hope it stays that way, although I'm not holding my breath. It's gonna get hot, really hot.' He sighed. 'That's what bothers me the most. At least there's air conditioning. That is, if I can find the remote control.'

'Shall I help you look?'

'Nah, it'll show up. I hope.' He flicked his head over his shoulder. 'What was going on out there by the way? Who was the skinny dude with the dog?'

Back out on the street, the Apothecary had been the one gripping Anaïs's shoulder. By chance his new post was hidden beneath the building they had been standing in front of. In the side street the Apothecary had ushered the group through the entrance of a real pharmacy. The shop was closed for the midday siesta and vacant. They were therefore not disturbed by the owners.

Hidden at the back between tiers of drawers in a storage room was a lift. It was similar to the one in Amsterdam. They had been transported down several floors. Anaïs, the Apothecary and Immi had practically frozen to death, crammed into the small lift with the two shades. Even now their body temperatures were fighting to return to normal levels.

Anaïs shivered involuntarily and not just from the cold. 'I honestly don't know who it is. We've met before. He first showed up in Amsterdam and has been chasing me ever since.' She thought for a moment. 'There was a sort of showdown in Cornwall and he disappeared. I assumed he was gone for good. Clearly, I was wrong.'

'Geez, Cornwall? You have been getting around.'

She flashed her eyes at him. 'I know. Tell me about it!'

'Well, you're safe now. They'll never find you here.' The Apothecary winked at her. 'I had enough trouble finding the place myself.'

Anaïs smiled. 'Good to know.'

The Apothecary turned his attention to her companions. He scratched his head again and looked at one of the shades.

'If you don't mind me asking, who's the cross-dresser?'

'Cross-dresser?' Anaïs was confused for a moment and then realised he was talking about Marilyn. 'Oh, her, ahem, him? Guess.'

'What is it? A him or a her? Give me a break. Why can't you just tell me?'

Anaïs was unmoved. 'Nope, guess.'

The Apothecary pursed his lips and ran his eyes over the shade. 'Conchita Wurst?'

Anaïs snorted. 'C'mon, you're not even trying.'

He cocked his head. 'Madonna?'

Anaïs blew a raspberry. 'Madonna? How could it be Madonna? She's still alive and kicking! So is Conchita. How many shades have you actually met?'

'Not a lot,' he said. 'It's not my department.'

'Fine, if you're not going to take it seriously I'll tell you.'

'Good,' he said and folded his arms. 'I hate games.'

'It's Marilyn, Marilyn Monroe,' said Anaïs proudly.

The Apothecary's jaw dropped and he stared wide-eyed at the shade. 'You're kidding!'

He straightened his lab coat, bowed and doffed his baseball cap. 'It's an honour to meet you, Miss Monroe. I'm a big fan.' He shuffled his feet nervously. 'I hope you don't mind me prying, but what was the whole deal with the Kennedys? I mean, did they really knock you off?'

Marilyn cleared her throat. *'Who is this imbecile?'*

'Don't mind him,' said Anaïs, shooting a glance at the shade. 'He's actually quite cool once you get to know him.'

'I doubt it.'

'What did she say?' enquired the Apothecary.

'Oh nothing,' said Anaïs. She hissed at him. 'I think it would be better if you didn't ask those sorts of questions.'

The Apothecary screwed up his mouth and pulled in his chin. 'Why? What's the problem? What did I say?'

'I don't think you should talk about the you-know-whos.'

'The you-know-whos?'

'My god, I didn't think you were that thick.' She stepped close to him and lowered her voice. 'The Kennedys.'

'Ah.'

'Don't talk about it. It's insensitive.'

The Apothecary tried to process the information. 'Ok, suit yourself. I was just curious.'

'What a moron!' Marilyn exclaimed.

Anaïs grabbed the shade's arm and spun her around. 'Maybe you better wait over there.' She indicated a couch positioned against the wall next to the lift doors. 'This won't take long.'

Marilyn hesitated and then obliged. She stomped across to the couch and sat down, simmering at the Apothecary.

He looked disconcertedly at the shade before turning to Anaïs. 'And what's up with the other cross-dresser?'

'Which one?'

'Her.' He pointed at the librarian.

'What!' exclaimed Immi. 'Cross-dresser?'

'Oops, sorry sister,' said the Apothecary, grinning. He raised his hands in defence. 'I was just having a bit of fun.'

The librarian regarded him with disdain.

He turned to Anaïs. 'I'll just shut up, shall I?'

'That might be wise,' said Anaïs. 'There is someone here you *do* know.'

Anaïs turned to her caretaker. 'This used to be Nan.'

'No!' The Apothecary shook his head in disbelief.

Anaïs looked at him sternly. 'Yes,' she said and nodded.

The Apothecary was genuinely upset and covered his mouth with his hand. 'I'm so sorry. I really liked her. She was hot,' he said through his fingers.

Anaïs glared at him. 'Are you trying to insult everyone in the room?' She shot a sideways glance at Nan.

'Sorry, that came out all wrong.' He was genuinely upset and sniffed. He avoided looking at Nan and took Anaïs by the arm. He pulled her close to him and whispered. 'That's terrible. What happened?'

'An accident,' said Anaïs flatly.

'Anaïs, I'm really sorry.' He turned to Nan. 'Are you all right?' There was a moment of silence. Getting no response from the shade he directed his attention back to Anaïs. 'Is she all right?'

The little witch didn't respond and stared at the floor.

The Apothecary took a deep breath, eyed the women and exhaled slowly. 'Sorry, stupid question.'

There was a pregnant pause.

'Apology accepted,' said Anaïs, deadpan.

The Apothecary took another deep breath and tried to break the impasse. 'By the way, you've really grown. I barely recognised you.'

The little witch's face clouded over. 'Yeah, don't remind me,' she said with hint of sadness.

The Apothecary removed his cap and rubbed his head. He kneaded the cap in his hands apprehensively and his eyes flicked over the small group of women.

He took another deep breath and straightened his back. 'So, enough chit-chat. Is there anything you would like? It's all pretty unfamiliar here but I'll see if I can find what you need.'

Anaïs shook herself out of her sullen mood and attempted a half-hearted smile. 'Thanks, we could use your help.'

The Apothecary brightened and beamed at her. 'Excellent! Your wish is my command. Always willing to be of service.'

'Good,' said Anaïs. 'Get us out of here.'

'That's a bit beyond me, but I have a solution,' said the Apothecary. 'I'll call my mother.'

ASSISTANCE

A naïs was taken aback. 'Son of a witch?'

'Yes,' said the Apothecary.

Anaïs was surprised and a little dismayed. The sudden news of the relationship had floored her. She temporarily forgot their present predicament. 'Why didn't you mention this earlier? That your mother was a witch.'

'It never occurred to me,' replied the Apothecary sheepishly and with a tinge of guilt. 'There was no reason to tell you, I suppose. Besides, how often do we see each other anyway?'

Anaïs considered him for a moment. Usually, the only contact she had with him was through email. They did have something in common. They both shared a passion for music. But when she thought about it, she really didn't know much about him. He supplied her with potions and such, but was more an acquaintance than anything else. She realised she didn't even know his name.

'I thought the Organisation would've told you,' said the Apothecary.

'Unfortunately, *they* don't tell me anything!' Anaïs retorted.

The Apothecary pulled a long face and eyed her forlornly. 'That's a pity. What's wrong with them? I'm sure it would help if they kept you in the loop.'

Anaïs wrung her hands and stared glumly at a black speck on the wall. She stiffened. 'Yes, it would. It would help a lot.' She looked down at her feet and sucked her bottom lip.

Nan moved across to her and put a hand on her shoulder. Anaïs didn't feel the chill. She was already numb.

'They wanted to protect you, Anaïs,' said the shade gently. *'It wouldn't help to tell you everything. Not right away, anyway. I tried to give you as much information as I could. But with some things, you first need to learn for yourself before you'll be able to understand what you're being told.'*

Anaïs sighed. She wasn't convinced. 'They could have told me this.'

'They could have, but would it really matter? Would it make a difference?' She knelt down beside the little witch. *'You have to know you were never alone. There was, and always is, someone watching over you.'*

Nan bent forward and tried to put her head in the witch's line of sight.

Anaïs stared past her at the floor. She refused to look Nan in the eye. She considered the caretaker's words. It occurred to her that what Nan said was true. In more ways than one she was not alone. She thought about the car that had followed them on the highway. She thought about the feeling she'd had after it had disappeared. The feeling she was being watched. She thought about the dark figure she had seen outside on the basilica's steeple. She was certainly not alone. What bothered her was not knowing what or who was watching over her. And whether they were there to protect or attack her.

Nan spoke softly. *'Trust me, Anaïs. You will know everything in good time.'*

The witch straightened and turned to her caretaker. Their faces were centimetres away from one another. So close Anaïs could feel Nan's icy aura.

'That's good to know, Nan,' she said, almost in a whisper. 'But I still think it's a bit strange. Like they don't trust me.' She ran her eyes around the underground room. It was a large, long space and not well lit. There were dark recesses in the walls and she couldn't make out the far end of the room. It was pitch black. The feeling she was being watched returned. It was palpable. She shivered. Nan retracted her hand from the witch's shoulder and stepped away from her.

The Apothecary crouched down on his haunches in front of the little witch.

'Look,' he said. 'She can help. I'll call my mother. She'll come. She always does.' He smiled at her. 'I don't know about the rest of them but she's dependable.'

Anaïs stopped eying the room over the Apothecary's shoulder. She looked at him morosely. 'But I can't get close to another witch. It's dangerous.'

'Not a problem,' he said. 'We'll work it out. There are ways around that.' He stood, pulled out his phone and unplugged the headphones which were slung around his neck. 'I'll call her straight away.'

A voice sounded in the darkness. 'That won't be necessary.'

Anaïs looked past the Apothecary. A tall, thin woman, decked out in an air hostess's uniform, stepped out of the shadows in the far corner of the room

'I am already here,' she said.

CHILDREN

naïs Blue was fortunate to have a rare gift that is only bestowed on children. When you are young, more magical things come to you. Anaïs had second sight. She could sense and feel things others could not. Naturals have this too but the skill is rarely retained and developed. Often it is lost completely. This was not the case for Anaïs. She was still learning. She had an advantage. Even though she was mentally in her late teens, her physical form still influenced her. Like all small children, a part of her had not yet been fully indoctrinated into the adult world.

If we, as adults, could recall the inner beauty of childhood and not be forced to conform to the false lessons our counsellors have taught us, the world would be a far richer place for all concerned. There is much to be said about this influence. The wisdom of age is a useful thing. Unfortunately, it utterly destroys innocence. This innocence, which some may call naivety, is required to maintain an open mind. Most adults have lost this to their own detriment.

Small children are not given the benefit of intelligence. They are not trusted with knowledge. Yet they are far more resilient than they are given credit for, and they are clever. Although filters are put in place to ensure their education does not have a long term derogatory effect on development, these filters are poorly implemented.

Due to this oversight, fully matured humans tend to carry the pains of their formative years around with them. They forget the good. The joys of childhood are masked. This affects every decision they make and warps their view of the world. For some, the negative completely obliterates the positive. It haunts them for the rest of their lives. For others, it never ends and continues into the beyond. They can no longer recall the innocence at the very beginning of their existence. The wrong sort of education gets in the way. It prevents them from truly having free thought.

If we were able to step out of these inbuilt restrictive zones and let fate hold our hands, we would get a great deal more out of life. I cannot deny that I too have fallen into this regimentation. But then, I am not a witch.

The Organisation is extremely careful on the behavioural development front. A heavy, but delicate hand had been dealt with Anaïs's education. Or perhaps it could be better described as mis-education. She had been sheltered to encourage free thought.

Witches must maintain an open mind. It is not

possible to influence other people successfully, or supernaturally, if your upbringing has been tainted. Quite simply, you can no longer see clearly. How on earth are you going to notice the little things? Stuff like the subtle changes in seasons, or that one fragile insect trying to make its way across a busy highway. It ends with opening your eyes and always starts with opening your mind.

As a child the world is an exciting place. Every day brings new discoveries. Imagination is given room to thrive. The outside world accepts odd behaviour and acting out fantasies. Children have enormous freedom. Witches make an effort to maintain this but sometimes, for them just as with all of us, life gets in the way.

If the training is successful, witches can cope with acquiring knowledge without losing the child within. There are distinct advantages to their slow physical growth. Each stage in their development is allowed to take its own sweet time. There is no hurry—no pressure. Not giving more information than is absolutely necessary is fundamental. This can be frustrating for the student. Every child constantly wants to know more. There is a desire to suck everything in as fast as possible. But we all need to find stable footing before we can fly.

Anaïs had been given the chance to play with magic before it needed to be put into practice. This concentrated effort on the part of her nurturers would stand her in good stead. The advantages of her prolonged early childhood had been fully harnessed and strengthened. If she relied on them and trusted her educators she would be a force to be reckoned with. She would know how to use her powers correctly.

We all have the chance to take advantage of childhood. We should never forget what we once were. Our inner child is the most important part of our psyche and should never be subdued or destroyed. It should be honed. Without it we can never fully be ourselves. When this part of us is lost we forget our place in the world. We lose our magic.

THE MOTHER

The uniform was bright blue. The sight of it made Anaïs cringe. The air hostess had long blonde hair which was tied up in a bun and sat like a crown upon her head. A thick layer of make-up coated her face, and her pencilled eyebrows were positioned unnaturally high on her forehead.

'How are you, Anaïs? It's so good to see you again,' she said.

Anaïs took a step away from her and screwed up her face. 'Again?'

She averted her eyes from the blue uniform and studied the woman's face. Anaïs guessed she was in her mid twenties, although it was difficult to discern. The make-up caked on her skin hid her true age.

'Yes, we've met before,' said the woman.

Anaïs frowned. 'We have?'

'Yes,' said the air hostess. 'We met in Amsterdam.'

'Oh?' Anaïs drew a blank. The woman was unfamiliar. Apart from that, Anaïs was still trying to work out how she could possibly be the Apothecary's mother. She was far too young.

'Do you remember the library?'

Anaïs eyed her suspiciously. 'Yes.'

She ran her mind back over the last few days. So much had happened. But she had not forgotten her experience in the library in the Rijksmuseum.

Anaïs stepped back in fear. 'Caput Mortuum!'

The witch had not been happy to see her then and probably would not be now. Without other members of the Organisation around to stop her, Caput Mortuum might be a threat. Anaïs sensed danger and grabbed Nan's arm. She pulled the shade in front of her. 'Don't hurt me. Look, I found your daughter.'

She quickly released her grip. Her hand throbbed in pain from the cold. She cupped her hands and blew hot breath into her palms. It did not have the desired effect and she shook her wrists vigorously to encourage the blood to flow.

Now it was the air hostess's turn to be confused. 'My daughter?' She shook her head. 'No, I don't think so.' She turned and indicated the librarian.

'This is my daughter,' she said.

Anaïs was nonplussed. Still convinced she was facing Caput Mortuum she stuttered, 'Yes … but isn't this your other one?'

'Other one? No, I don't have another one. One is definitely more than enough.' She threw a disapproving eye over the librarian. Immi reddened, her usual bravado completely gone. She shrank away from the woman and made herself small. Cut down in size she looked like a little girl. The air hostess moved over to the librarian and attempted to give her a kiss.

Immi ducked away from her, and yelped. 'Oh, Mum, not now! Give it a rest!'

Anaïs was dumbstruck. She knotted her brow and gaped at the two women.

The air hostess began to fuss over the librarian. 'Why do you insist on wearing such a warm coat in this weather? You aren't in England any more.'

'I like it,' said Immi defensively and wrapped her arms around her chest.

Anaïs cried out in bewilderment. 'Hang on!' She eyeballed the librarian. 'Wait a minute. This really is your mother?'

The librarian turned up her lip. 'Yes, I'm afraid so.'

Anaïs shook her head and tried to process the information.

'But then ...' she spluttered. 'Then, you're his sister!' She pointed and waved a finger at the Apothecary.

The librarian didn't look at her brother but cocked her head towards her mother. 'Maybe it would be better if she explained it.'

'Somebody better start explaining something,' said Anaïs, fuming.

The high-pitched peals of Marilyn's laughter cut through her skull. Anaïs slapped her hands around her head. 'Aah!' she cried.

'This just gets more entertaining all the time!' Marilyn chirped. *'I like you people. You're a riot. I think I'll stick around.'*

Anaïs spun around, glared at the shade and snarled, 'Get out of my head!'

Marilyn sank deep into the couch and raised her hands in defence. *'Sorry I opened my mouth.'*

The air hostess waved her arms and beckoned for calm, 'Why don't we all settle down?'

Anaïs was confused. 'If you are not Caput Mortuum, then who are you?'

'I am Sojourner Pink,' said the air hostess. 'I thought you knew about me.' She turned to the librarian. 'Didn't you explain it to her?'

Immi hunched her shoulders. 'A little,' she said.

Sojourner Pink scrunched up her face in annoyance. Her make-up cracked. She shot a dark look at her daughter. She inhaled deeply through her nose and looked down at the little witch. 'Anaïs, I was given the task to find out what happened to you in Amsterdam. Do you remember now?'

Anaïs scratched her head and grunted, 'Vaguely.'

She thought for a moment. Then the conversation she had with the librarian in the Morris Minor came back to her. With all that had happened in between it was not surprising she had forgotten. But how could she forget about the witch with the really cool name? And Sojourner Pink had stood by her. She was the only one who had tried to defend her in the presence of Caput Mortuum.

Anaïs nodded. 'I remember now. You took me by surprise and, well, I didn't recognise you.'

'I understand,' said Sojourner, looking down at her uniform. 'I had to borrow another body.'

'Another body?'

'You do know that we can do this,' said Sojourner. 'Take possession of a natural.'

'Yes, I know. I wish I could do that,' said Anaïs, running her eyes over Sojourner.

'You will learn in time, Anaïs.'

The little witch nodded slowly.

'So we are clear? You know who I am?'

'I don't know everything, but yes, now I know who you are.' Anaïs tilted her head towards the librarian. 'She did tell me.'

'Good,' said Sojourner. She eyed her daughter and glanced around the room. Spying Marilyn on the couch she gave the shade a stern look. 'I see you are still up to your antics.'

The shade shrugged.

Anaïs gawped at the witch and then at Marilyn.

The shade batted her eyelids. *I told you, you were not the first one I'd met.*

Anaïs overcame her initial surprise. Marilyn had indeed said she had met other witches.

Sojourner turned her attention to Nan. 'And who is this, then? The one you claimed was my daughter.'

Anaïs looked uncomfortably at her caretaker and then at the witch. She cleared her throat.

'This is Nan,' she said softly.

It was now Sojourner's turn to be taken aback. The pencilled eyebrows jumped on her forehead. She stared at the shade in astonishment.

Anaïs gave her caretaker a nudge. 'Tell her, Nan,' she said.

AN ESCAPE PLAN

'I'm so glad you have been found, Nan,' said Sojourner. 'What a relief. We were very upset when we heard what had happened.'

'I can imagine,' said the caretaker flatly.

Sojourner lacked the second-sight of Anaïs's sunglasses but it was clear from Nan's tone that she was not at all happy to see another witch. Even if they were there to help.

'I am truly sorry, Nan. This should never have happened,' said Sojourner gently. 'We will work it out. I honestly have no idea what we will do, but we will find a solution. Your mother was very upset.'

She looked Nan in the eye, but they were dead even to her.

'I'll survive,' murmured the shade. *'And please, don't mention my mother!'*

Nan practically spat the last sentence. Sojourner fiddled nervously with the lapels of her uniform. 'The main thing is you are still here. You are one of us, Nan.

Your survival is of utmost importance. It has, and always will be, our job to protect. Above all, we never sacrifice our own.'

'A lot of good that does me now.'

Anaïs moved between her caretaker and Sojourner. She fixed the witch with a steely glare.

'Nan will be fine,' said Anaïs defiantly. 'She is with me.'

The older witch frowned at Anaïs. Then her face mellowed. She looked down at her with a mixture of sadness and concern. 'I know you want to help, Anaïs. But I don't think you have the expertise to solve this problem.'

'We will see about that,' said Anaïs with determination.

Sojourner gave her a stern look. 'I can understand that you're upset, Anaïs, but you must trust us. We are here to help.'

The little witch was unconvinced. 'You or someone else from the Organisation should have come to see me earlier. Maybe then this wouldn't have happened.'

'Perhaps,' said Sojourner. They all fell silent. Sojourner glanced furtively from the little witch to the shade.

'We will deal with Nan later,' she said. 'Right now, we have a more immediate problem to solve. You are in danger here, Anaïs.' She glanced around the room. 'You are all in danger. I understand there is the situation with your promptuary, Anaïs. Without it you will not have the necessary protection.'

'How do you know about my promptuary?'

'We have ears,' said Sojourner.

'I'm afraid to ask whose ears those would be,' said Anaïs. She glanced at the librarian.

The older witch chose not to respond to her comment. She smoothed down the front of her uniform. She tilted her head towards the Apothecary. 'Hamish here will make the arrangements.'

Anaïs grinned at the Apothecary. 'Hamish?'

The Apothecary grimaced and turned bright red. He scratched the stubble on his chin. 'I prefer Hank if you don't mind.'

'I'm not surprised,' said Anaïs and chortled. 'Hamish!'

Sojourner frowned. 'Enough of this! We don't have a lot of time. Whoever is chasing you will not be held back for long by a child's trick.'

Anaïs stopped smiling and cleared her throat. 'What do you propose?'

'You will need to get to Italy,' said Sojourner. 'That's where your handbook can be repaired.'

'Ok, but how are we supposed to get there?'

'You will do as everyone else does,' said Sojourner. 'Use modern magic and fly.'

THE AIRPORT

Anaïs took one last look at the Morris Minor. She was sorry to leave it behind. It had become an integral part of their little company. Most of all she would miss the music. It was the Morris Minor's secret weapon. The car instinctively knew how to shut everyone up, particularly the librarian. Although imbued with special talents, Anaïs knew it was just a piece of machinery. It did have a personality, but it wasn't a person. Yet, of all her travelling companions, the car was the one she could best relate to. Just like her, it was small, tenacious and independent. It could also get its way if it wanted.

The car regarded her with its headlights. It wasn't really looking at her, or was it? The bug-shaped headlamps were a little too intense for her liking. Anaïs averted her eyes from them. She moved closer to the car and stood beside the front wheel well. She ran her hand slowly over the curve of fender, practically stroking it. The heat of the engine filtering through the metal was warm like a body. Reluctantly she retracted her hand and turned away from the car. She went to walk across to the entrance to the airport terminal when a movement caught her eye. She sucked in her breath and held it.

There he was again, standing defiantly on the curb on the other side of the road—the shade with the thick-lensed spectacles. The same one who had stopped her on the streets of Amsterdam. What was it with this guy? And how had he got here? He was certainly persistent. She had to give him that much. As far as she was concerned, he could try all he wanted but what she did was her business. Right now she had her hands full anyway. He would have to get in line.

He didn't move. *Good, let him stand there for all eternity. Ok, maybe that's a bit unfair.* She was supposed to help them. Only this one was far too pushy. *What was it he wanted again?* There was something about a girl. He had drawn her name in chalk on the footpath. *Yes, that was it.* She looked at the ground and tried to visualise the letters he had written. *Julia, that was her name. Julia.* Well, right now he could take his Julia and shove it. She had more important things to do.

She stopped staring at the pavement. She raised her head and looked across the road. He was gone. Strange. An involuntary shiver ran up her spine. Even with her knowledge of the world this was eerie. Shades just don't disappear of their own accord. *Forget it. Get a move on. If he really wants help, he'll be back.* She looked around. There was nobody, just her and the Morris Minor. *Where was everybody anyway? It was an airport. Shouldn't it be busy?* She took a deep breath and exhaled through her nose. *Pull yourself together.* She turned to face the entrance to the terminal. She clenched her fists and marched across to it.

The moment she moved through the revolving doors she felt it, a chill in the air. Outside it was unseasonably warm, the mercury creeping above twenty degrees centigrade. Inside was a different matter. The drop in temperature came not just from the air conditioning, which blasted down at her from an outlet above the door, but something else. Her core body warmth dissolved. The cold cut her to the bone.

Anaïs walked further into the terminal and looked around. It was busy. She spied the librarian nervously standing in a corner, trying to remain inconspicuous in the company of the two shades. Immi had no cause to worry. The shades were not alone. Anaïs pulled off her beret and stuck her hand into it. Feeling around she found what she was looking for. She donned her sunglasses and scanned the expansive entry hall. There were shades everywhere.

A woman with a child in her arms hovered lethargically by a set of turnstiles. There were others. Tourists dressed for the beach, some in board shorts and bikinis, looked out of place dressed in their summer garb in such chilly conditions. An elderly man in a hospital gown trailed a multitude of plastic tubes, as if he had recently got up and walked away from his bed, presumably deserting his life support system. There were many more. They stood hovering on their shadowless spots. Living, breathing commuters wended their way between them, the naturals oblivious to what they were in the midst of.

Anaïs slid the sunglasses down to the tip of her nose. She peered over them. With their camouflages holding firm, the shades blended easily into the crowd. Apart from the fact they were static, there was nothing visually unusual about them. The naturals in the terminal were too intent on getting to their destinations to pay any attention to them. For the shades it was different. They had no destination. They had no choice. They were going nowhere.

Anaïs pushed the sunglasses back up her nose. *How am I supposed to get through this?* She scanned the hall for any telltale signs that she had been noticed. She reassured herself. *You'll be fine. Just act normal, whatever that means.* She assumed the air of a harried traveller and stomped defiantly across the hall to her companions.

As she sidled up to them, the librarian smirked at her gait. 'What's wrong with you?'

She hissed loudly through her teeth at the librarian. 'Let's get out of here before I'm spotted.'

'Why? Are we in danger?' Immi's eyes flitted around the entry hall.

Anaïs lowered her voice, speaking out of the corner of her mouth. 'You aren't, but I could find myself dealing with some unwanted attention.' She pointed at her sunglasses. 'We have company.'

The librarian glanced furtively around the hall again. 'Really? Where?'

'Everywhere,' said Anaïs. 'And I mean literally,

everywhere. More than half of the people you see here are not alive.'

'Oh?' The librarian swallowed hard.

'Let's just go.'

Immi nodded.

Anaïs turned to her own shades. 'Are you two coming?'

'*Yes!*' Marilyn and Nan chimed in unison.

'Good, then let's try and get to the plane.'

'*How are we going to do that?*' asked Nan.

'Sojourner said she would solve it. We just have to find her. If not, we're stranded.' She scanned the terminal in search of the other witch. 'Although, I suppose if all else fails we could get back in the car.'

'No, anything but that,' said the librarian in mild panic. 'I've had my fill of magic cars. No offence, but if I have to drive, I much prefer to be in control of where I'm going. Let's just get moving.'

Immi ushered Nan and Marilyn together and pushed them in front of her. She then slapped her hands together, rubbed them vigorously and cupped her palms. She blew warm air into them. 'You guys are freezing!'

The shades looked at each other and shrugged. Immi pulled her arms up into her sleeves and gave them another shove. 'Come on, you two, this way.'

MOVING SHADES

You may recall that previously I tried to explain to you the complications associated with getting around as a shade. One of the things I mentioned was the difficulties presented by various forms of transport. I specifically discussed the inability to control or pilot a vehicle of any description. I also related the situation of trying to get someone else to be the pilot. In the end the only real solution is to get yourself a witch.

At one stage I delved into the problem of air travel. Flying continent to continent is nigh on impossible for a shade. You need a passport, and they require things such as photographs and fingerprints. The photograph is an impossibility, if you cannot be seen. Or if you are barely there. Film will only record something that is truly physical.

Photography itself is a kind of magic. Especially if you have never encountered it before. Technology in the past two centuries has moved forward at such a fast pace. In the beginning the natural world had trouble keeping up. So many wonders occurred. Naturals could not judge what was real and what was not. They were flooded with all kinds of new and fantastic developments. One of those things was the advancement of transportation. Another was photography.

During the early days of photography there were those who attempted to use this new technology to prove the existence of the spirit world. The camera was the chosen form of proof for many unexplained occurrences. For some reason we are more willing to believe the lens than what we see with our naked eye.

One instance of an attempt to capture the unknown was the Cottingley Fairies. Two girls in the early twentieth century took photographs of themselves with what they purported to be little winged people. They managed to convince themselves and everyone else for sixty years that what they had recorded was real. In the end they owned up to fabricating the photographs. However, by that stage, because they had sworn blind to this fallacy for so long, they were less than convinced of what the truth actually was. They believed their own lie.

Film also has a mind of its own, and what we try to harness could in fact be harnessing us. What we see with our eyes can fool us most of the time. Particularly if it is something we truly want to believe is real. Sometimes we should pay more attention to our instincts and ignore our fantastical desires.

Ancient cultures have always had trouble accepting an image created by a camera. There is the impression that something put onto film is removing a part of the soul. They may not be that far wrong. If you take a look at Hollywood cinema actors, it's very clear something drains from them over time. The longer they are in front of the camera, the less three-dimensional they become. Quite often, towards the end of their careers, there's very little left except a shell of their former selves. They almost become shades.

The development of photography, and in particular film, would not have advanced so precipitously if it hadn't been for witches. Witches had this form of magic harnessed centuries ago. The promptuary would only serve a small part of its purpose if it was reduced to merely providing static images. Once again, someone did not keep this information to themselves. The result has been quite astounding. A whole industry has now gestated and grown out of this magical process. The moving picture has become the number one manner of communication in modern society. So much so, it is slipping to the point where physical face-to-face interaction is on the decline. But I digress. We were discussing the intricacies of powered flight.

Owing to the limitations of non-existent photographic images intercontinental flight is impossible for shades. This does not mean they cannot use this form of transport at all. The European mainland has open borders. This provides a golden opportunity for shade conveyance. It means that if a shade can book a seat and get through metal detectors, then they can fly. Lacking ready access to a ticket booking system is a problem. However, metal detectors are not a major obstacle. They are not designed to detect the supernatural and therefore reasonably easy to fool if you do not physically exist, although most shades are unaware of this.

Of course, some kind of identification is still required at the start of your journey. Any apothecary worth their salt is skilled at manipulating images. Forging documents for witches is one prerequisite for the job.

If all of these complications can be overcome, then the only barrier is perhaps strip-searching. Thankfully, that doesn't go on as often any more. Touching another person is considered an invasion of privacy and could land you in court. Security personnel may have a job to do but usually are not paid enough to take the risk.

Freedom of movement for a shade is not impossible, but they still need help and a successful diversion. A shade in the know can go places, particularly one with a witch in tow.

BORDER CONTROL

The security guards were all due for a coffee break. Some of them were on the frayed edge of nicotine deprivation, treading a fine line between curbing their irritation and fighting to maintain concentration. Putting on a smiling face for hours on end leads to muscle fatigue. Their faces ached. Every new passenger had become a number that had to be shuffled through the security process as quickly as possible.

The personnel at Barcelona's El Prat International Airport had rotated their positions so many times nobody knew exactly what they should be doing any more. Their automatic pilots had kicked in.

The guy staring at the infrared screen could no longer tell what shade of grey he was looking at. Or what shape corresponded to what common everyday object. Was that a legless Barbie doll or an Uzi? Was that bottle of shampoo under, or over, the legal limit? Was that an electric toothbrush or an implement for sexual gratification? How many books was this person really going to read on their holiday and why hadn't they been introduced to a lightweight electronic alternative? How much dehydrated soup did a person really need? *Wait, a potato peeler?*

He held up his hand and his supervisor came to inspect if it was a weapon of mass destruction. The supervisor squinted at the screen and decided to err on the side of caution. Anything was better than being responsible for letting the wrong passenger through. Especially one who had the potential to bore a blunt kitchen utensil into someone's jugular. The risk outweighed the inconvenience, even if it meant sorting through a bag full of three-day-old socks.

The woman manning the electronic body sweeper had forgotten to refresh the batteries. She waved the device up and down a passenger's body and it bleeped feebly. The bulge in his pants certainly looked dangerous. She swept him again and decided not to investigate further. It was not the first time that day she had inadvertently groped something that she wished she had not. She waved him through. She turned her attention back to the walk-through metal detector and waited for the next passenger. She placed a hand on her hip, absentmindedly picked something out of her teeth, cast her arm over her shoulder and scratched a hard-to-reach spot on her spine with the wand. Her nicotine levels were borderline.

Anaïs assessed her shades. They had no luggage and were not wearing coats so they should be fine. She crossed her fingers and hoped that neither of them would be required to take off their shoes. Marilyn had found a way to manipulate her camouflage, but Anaïs was unsure if she could actually take anything off. Her stilettos could cause a problem, not to mention those Immi was wearing. The librarian would not be a problem. She could remove clothing. She could also respond to the directives issued by the guards. The shades could not.

Anaïs went first. She strolled as nonchalantly as possible through the full-body metal detector. It beeped and a light shone halfway up the display on its rim. The woman with the wand waved the instrument at Anaïs and shooed her back through the machine.

'Take off your hat, please!' commanded the woman brusquely.

Anaïs did as she was told. The woman's curt tone irritated her, but she thought better of making a scene. They had to get through with as little fuss as possible. She stepped back through the detector and placed her beret in the plastic container provided. She watched it being fed along the rollers and felt a twinge of apprehension as it disappeared into the scanner. All her earthly possessions were in it, including the promptuary. Could they see through it? She watched the face of the man studying the screen. It lit up his bored countenance. He stared vacantly at the x-ray images. His supervisor prodded him and his eyes came back to life and zipped over the screen.

The woman with the wand bent forward. Resting her hands on her thighs she narrowed her eyes and looked through the metal detector at the little witch. She beckoned Anaïs towards her. 'Come on,' she said impatiently. She cast an eye on the clock on the wall and cursed under her breath. She needed a break. Where was her replacement?

Anaïs stepped back into the detector and was ushered through to the other side. There were no telltale beeps or buzzes. The woman swept her up and down with the wand and sent her to get her stuff. Her attention turned to the others in their motley crew. Nan went first. There was no reaction from the full-body detector. The lights on the leading edge of the machine which should have turned green, failed to register. This was not surprising as there was nothing physical to detect. The woman stepped forward and thumped the side of the detector. She twirled her finger, indicating that Nan should walk through again. She obliged. Again, there was no response.

The woman huffed in exasperation and swept the shade with her wand. There was no reaction from the implement.

'Grandma?' Anaïs called out to her caretaker. 'Can you help me with my hat?'

The guard looked first at the little witch and then back at Nan. She decided the older woman was harmless and flicked her thumb, indicating the caretaker was free to go. She turned to scan her next victim. Her eyes widened at the sight of Marilyn. She cleared her throat.

'This way please,' she said with her voice cracking.

The security guard had met all sorts in her job but never someone like this. A bearded man, in a pin-striped suit wearing stilettos and heavy make-up, was not something she had to deal with on a daily basis. She did her best to conceal her surprise and maintain an ingenuous attitude. She failed dismally. She bit her lower lip in an effort to control her facial expressions. Her face quivered with the effort.

The shade stepped through the detector. This time there was a reaction from the machine. A red light shone on the side console midway up the shade's body. Anaïs guessed the compact in Marilyn's jacket had set it off. The guard opened her mouth to direct Marilyn back through the apparatus but was interrupted.

'Miss Wurst,' said Sojourner Pink. 'I've been looking for you everywhere.'

The witch stepped between the guard and Marilyn. Sojourner was still in possession of the hostess's body and assumed the air of someone going about her everyday business. The guard eyed her quizzically.

'Excuse me, we have an honoured guest,' said Sojourner. 'Do you mind?'

The guard was mildly affronted but decided against any action. She shook her head silently. She was unsure how to deal with such a strange personage anyway and secretly pleased she would not have to.

'It's … Ahem, *they're* all yours,' said the guard. She sniffed and cleared her throat again.

'Thank you for your co-operation,' said Sojourner. She waved her hand towards an electric airport baggage car. 'This way, madam.'

Marilyn obliged and walked across to the vehicle, her heels clicking loudly on the tiled floor. The guard followed her movement with a mixture of incredulity and amusement. Sojourner thanked the guard once more and followed the shade.

They all piled into the little electric car and waited for the librarian. Their progress was further slowed by her. Immi was sent through the detector several times and was gradually forced to strip to her bare essentials. In due course she was passed, but was then asked to empty her oversized handbag of all its contents.

Eventually, Immi was cleared. She donned her clothing, stuffed her belongings back into her handbag and shuffled across to the car.

Sojourner tapped her fingers on the baggage car's steering wheel. She furrowed her brow and scowled at her daughter. 'Hurry up and get in. We will miss the flight.'

TAKE-OFF

Anaïs had chosen to sit between the two shades. She couldn't rely on the librarian to cover for them in the event pertinent questions were asked. She had wrapped herself as snuggly as possible. Low-cost airlines don't have the benefit of ample leg room or broad seats. People practically sit on top of one another, crammed in like the proverbial sardines in a can. Even though Anaïs was small she was still forced to rub shoulders with her shades.

It was very uncomfortable. She was freezing. Anaïs stood on her seat and opened the air-conditioning jets on the console above her. She directed all three of them down on her seat. She could put up with the wind as long as it could regulate the temperature. The air-conditioning was not working. Even though it was warmer than the shades, it barely cut through the deathly cold.

She made a mental note to ask Sojourner if there was any way she could provide herself with some protection against it. She expected her promptuary could tell her, if she could get it fixed. The other option was to ask the Organisation or send a message to the Apothecary. But, again, she would need a fully operational promptuary. It would have to wait. There was nothing she could do about it now except grin and bear it, which was literally what she was doing. She clamped her teeth together in order to stop them chattering.

'Guys, I'm really cold,' said Anaïs through her teeth. 'Do you think you could give me a little bit more room.'

Both shades leaned away from her but were restricted by their seats. Anaïs checked if any of the other passengers were watching and then took off her beret and felt around inside. She pulled out a pair of purple mittens and a scarf. She then stuck her hand back in the beret and searched around inside. She noticed Marilyn watching her with wide eyes.

'*What are you doing?*'

'I'm cold,' said Anaïs.

'*I meant, what's with your arm?*'

Anaïs had reached so deeply, her arm had disappeared all the way up to her shoulder. 'Oh this? It's where I keep all my stuff.'

'*Handy,*' said Marilyn. '*But how do you find anything in it?*'

'I just focus. Usually whatever it is jumps into my hand.'

'*Unless your mind wanders and you end up with a half-eaten chicken burger,*' quipped Nan.

'That's only happened once,' said Anaïs with indignation. 'I don't put food in there any more.'

'I know,' said Nan. *'I was just winding you up.'*

Anaïs frowned at the shade. Marilyn cocked her head, not having understood what the little witch was talking about.

'Got it!' Anaïs exclaimed, grinning with delight. She extracted her arm and the fur-lined collar of a jacket appeared clenched in her fist. She set the beret on the floor between her feet and stood on the edges of it. She grunted and wrenched at the jacket. She bit her lip and pulled with all her might. After a struggle a heavily padded winter anorak emerged through the small opening. Marilyn's eyes widened even further.

Anaïs put on the coat, scarf and mittens. It helped but she still felt the frosty aura of the shades seeping through. As soon as the plane took off she decided she would get up and walk around—if possible, for most of the flight. There was no way she could put up with the cold for an extended period. She was relatively certain they wouldn't be bothered much. The airline would only give away the bare minimum and if you wanted anything more than a cup of coffee you would be charged extra. Low cost flying does not come without a price.

Anaïs reached over and clicked in the shades seat belts before doing up her own. The airliner trundled across the apron away from the terminal and out onto a taxiway. They coasted along for some time before being stuck waiting in a long queue of aircraft. Presently the other planes before them took off. The plane moved onto the main runway and positioned itself for take-off.

Anaïs wondered if Sojourner would be there to meet them when they arrived at their destination. She had not been able to board with them and said she would join them later. She could not use the air hostess's body for too long. It was not beyond her magical capabilities. Although possession did require an enormous amount of energy there were other problems. A host could not survive for very long in stasis. It was detrimental to their health for one thing. Dumping one in a foreign country with no idea where they were was also not considered kosher. Procuring a suitable new host would take time.

The engines began to roar and Anaïs felt the vibrations running through the entire aircraft. She felt her hand suddenly plummet in temperature. She looked down. Marilyn had taken a firm grip of it and squeezed her little hand. Even the mitten could not provide much protection. Anaïs looked up at the shade's face. Without her sunglasses, and even through the camouflage, Anaïs could see the fear in the shade's eyes.

'What's wrong? Are you ok?'

'No not really.' Marilyn shook her head. *'It's been a while since I've flown. When I last travelled jet airliners were relatively new. Also, I've been looking up. The sky seems to be full of them. Is it safe?'*

'So they say. Safer than driving is what they like to remind you.'

'Yes, I've heard that before. It still doesn't instil me with much confidence. I'd rather stay on the ground.'

'A bit late now,' said Anaïs. 'And you're dead. What is there to be afraid of anyway?'

Before the shade could answer they were both pressed into their seats. Marilyn squeezed her hand even harder and let out a long scream. Thankfully none of the other passengers could hear it. Anaïs could, and wrapped her free arm around her head. Unsurprisingly, it didn't help.

Great! Another journey with some nutcase. Anaïs thought, glancing over at the librarian seated across the aisle. *Please stop!*

TURBINE TORTURE

The aircraft was buffeted by crosswinds as it
rumbled to the end of the tarmac and lifted
off. Once it gained some elevation it dipped its
wings. As it banked sharply, Anaïs had a clear view of
the airport through the window. She choked on her
breath.

Beneath her she could make out a dark figure
standing in the open on the terminal's apron. It wasn't
alone. Beside it was another four-legged shadow—a
huge dog. Even from where she was, Anaïs could clearly
see the animal tugging on its invisible chain.

The aircraft slowly circled the airport. In the minute
or so it took to do this Anaïs watched in fascination as a
curious exchange took place.

The Inquisitor watched the plane turn and follow the
perimeter of the airfield. He pivoted his body, following

the movement of the aircraft, and considered his options. He could bring it down if he was quick. It was risky, but if he let it go he would have to start all over again, which would only delay the inevitable. He would get them but he was tired of all the chasing. He was irritated and losing his patience.

It had taken quite some time to extract himself from his paper prison. He could still taste the dust in his mouth. He smacked his lips. There was also the pasty hint of poster glue on his palate. Worst of all, he stank. He was actually far beyond irritated. He was plain pissed off.

He slipped his free hand into the inside pocket of his coat and extracted his handbook. *Let's see if this works.* He clutched the hound's chain tighter in his hand and adjusted his grip. The dog yanked at its invisible leash and in turn at his arm. He glared at it in frustration.

'Still!' he yelled at the hound.

The animal looked up at him. Its red eyes flared. It whined and reluctantly stopped straining against its bindings. The claws of one enormous paw scratched impatiently at the asphalt. The Inquisitor looked up at the clouds. He shut out the sound of the dog. He straightened his free arm and held the book above his head. He stared at it and breathed in deeply through his nostrils. They twitched, detecting his own putrid odour and that of the dog. He slowly dropped his arm and aimed it at the circling aircraft.

He closed his eyes and whispered to himself. *Focus.*

Then it hit him, a force from behind. It lifted him up and sent him flying forwards. He would have been blown further had it not been for the chain in his hand. The leash snapped taut. The dog anchored him to the ground. The arm attached to the chain became an extension of it. He heard his shoulder pop. He snapped his teeth together. His entire body whipped around, rotating on the joint. He smacked the ground hard, landing outstretched and spread-eagled full on his face. It took the wind out of him. He groaned and pulled his free arm under his body. He shook his head to clear it and tried to force air back into his lungs, panting. He used his arm to lever himself off the ground and scrabbled onto his hands and knees.

There was another blast of wind. This one was not directed at him but he felt its strong current flow over him. He snapped his eyes open and watched with fascination as a collection of loose stones lifted into the air before him. They were not alone. A short distance away the hound also became airborne. It flew towards him and he ducked as it soared over his head. As it passed over his body his shoulder was wrenched again. This time he cried out in agony. Once again his arm followed the leash. The force flipped him onto his back. The rest of him went with his damaged limb, dragged along the tarmac behind the hound. He scissored his legs and flipped himself back onto his stomach. He pulled up his knees and tried to slow himself. The rough surface of the runway cut through his thick trousers. The excruciating pain caused him to involuntarily drop the book and let his legs fall behind him.

The animal found purchase with its claws and halted its own movement. The Inquisitor continued sliding towards it. He twisted his body and tumbled until the solid legs of the hound stopped him. He came to a sudden halt under its muzzle. The dog drooled hot saliva. It dripped on his face and seared into his skin. Had it not been for this he may have passed out from the throbbing pain from his shoulder and damaged knees.

He shook his head, wiped his face with his sleeve and glanced around desperately. He found what he was looking for. He clawed at the ground and pulled himself towards it. He slapped his free hand down on the book. He wrapped his fingers around its spine and pulled it to his chest.

Arching his neck, he looked further afield. His heart sank. There it was again.

Anaïs's heart was beating fast. She had watched him fly through the air and come crashing down on the tarmac. It looked painful. The hound had flown over him and she had watched it turn itself in midair, almost cat-like, and land on all fours. It slid a few metres along the ground, dragging the Inquisitor with it, and stopped. The man's body went from sliding to rolling before colliding with the animal. She watched his head lift. He grappled for the object he had dropped. Then he froze, looking at something on the far side of the apron. She followed his gaze.

From between the aircraft parked at the terminal another figure in black appeared. It paced with purposeful determination towards the crumpled Inquisitor. It held something in both hands and directed it towards the man and his dog. He looked beaten.

Then her view was obscured. The airliner gained altitude and they were swallowed up by the cloud cover. Anaïs saw no more.

INFLIGHT

Marilyn pressed the little witch. *'Are you all right?'*

'Yes,' said Anaïs. 'Well, actually no. I just saw something.'

The shade studied the little witch's face. *'You look worried.'*

'I am.' Anaïs squirmed in her seat. 'Didn't you see it?'

'No.'

'You're sitting at the window,' said Anaïs. 'You should have seen it. It was down there on the runway,'

'I wasn't looking out the window.' Marilyn turned and watched white wisps of cloud swirl on the other side of the glass. *'I had my eyes closed. To be perfectly honest when we took off it freaked the hell out of me.'*

'I gathered that.' Anaïs looked down at the shade's hands. During take-off Anaïs had managed to free herself from the shade's grip. She had transferred Marilyn's hand to something that could cope with the cold. The shade still gripped the plastic armrests so intensely the whites of her knuckles shone through her camouflage.

'You can let go,' said Anaïs, nodding at her hand. 'We won't be landing for a while.'

Marilyn looked down. *'Oh, yeah.'* She released her grip and flexed her fingers.

'He was there again with his dog,' said Anaïs.

'Who?'

'The guy you pointed out to us back in the city. The one we saw on the street when we first met.'

'Oh him? I wouldn't worry about him.'

Anaïs snorted. 'How can you not worry about that?'

'I told you before, they don't bother me. I always get away.'

'That may be so, but I'm not sure you'll be able to do that forever.' Anaïs rubbed her eyes. The stark whiteness of the cloud outside half blinded her. She squinted and looked up at Marilyn. 'You seem pretty blasé about it. I've seen what they can do. Aren't you afraid of them?'

The shade sighed. *'Child, if I spent my time being afraid I would have no time to enjoy life.'*

Anaïs screwed up her face. 'You seemed pretty afraid before. And you're not alive.'

'Ok, you have a point. But I don't know a better way to describe it.' Marilyn twisted in her seat and looked down her nose at the little witch. *'Listen, I've experienced enough in my time to know you should be happy with what you've been given. Believe me, it doesn't get any better than what you have right now. This particular moment is all you have. You should live it to the full. You can't waste time worrying about what might be. You*

never know what will come or if you'll have a chance to do it anyway.'

'But you were someone really famous. You got there with hard work, didn't you? It didn't just come of its own accord. You had to work at it.'

'Sure, but fame is fleeting. And I'm not convinced it's worth all the effort. It's ok once you have it, but I'm telling you, maintaining it is not easy. Anyway, I wasn't referring to fame. I'm just saying you shouldn't worry about stuff in general.'

'Ok, then I'll try not to worry. I'm not convinced I shouldn't though.' Anaïs furrowed her brow. 'Whoever it was down there is not going to stop until they have what they want.'

'And do you know what that is?'

Anaïs shook her head.

'Then why worry? That's his problem. He's the one who has to worry about whatever it is that he has to get done, not you.' Marilyn elbowed Anaïs in the upper arm. *'You'll cope when the time comes.'*

Anaïs rubbed her arm. She reached out and played with the latch on her tray table. 'I suppose you're right.'

The shade settled into her seat and looked around the cabin.

'I'm puzzled,' said Anaïs. 'How do you know all this stuff? Not what you just told me, but everything. Like who you are. How do you remember? The last shade I met had no idea who he was.'

'I'm not sure,' said Marilyn. *'I like to exercise my mind. I always did. I used to read heaps. All kinds of stuff. I guess it helped.'* She gave Anaïs another nudge. *'And I'm a woman. I have a memory like an elephant.'*

Anaïs smirked. 'That could be a curse as much as a benefit.' She pulled a serious face. 'Sometimes I wish I could forget.'

Marilyn nodded and stared out the window. The aircraft had climbed above the clouds. The sun hit the fuselage and winked off the wings. It lit up the white mattress beneath them.

'*Me too,*' she said.

AIRBORNE

People will tell you time travel doesn't exist. They lie. It's easy and it's everywhere. It is a relatively new development but accessible to all. Anyone with a bit of pocket change can do it in principle. Some people do it daily. Most call it flying, but if you think about it you are actually travelling through time.

It will come as no surprise that witches played a significant role in the development of powered flight. Not specifically the getting airborne part. Naturals have had an obsession with becoming birds since time immemorial. This has been much to their own detriment. The human body is in no way constructed for flight. It is pretty good at falling, though. Witches merely intervened to prevent further carnage. Naturals need to be protected from themselves more than anything else. That's a full-time job in itself.

Witches decided enough was enough and gifted the

Wright brothers with the relatively simple concept of a steering mechanism. Flying is one thing. Anybody can do that. Crashing was the thing that needed to be avoided in order to make the short-lived thrill of soaring through the air less painful.

Once gifted this small device to prevent undue harm, naturals continued further in their endeavour to conquer the sky. The drive to fly higher and faster has developed to a point where they can now warp time. Even witches did not see that one coming.

Intercontinental flight is like space travel. It's otherworldly. In some ways it's interstellar. Whenever I flew I would go to where one of those huge doors were, usually at the back of the aircraft. You can lie over the bulkhead and look out through the window. You can shut out your surroundings and the cabin around you. You are in a cocoon.

I would press my nose up to the window. My entire head would feel as if it was almost outside the aircraft. I could even feel the cold. Outside it's minus fifty degrees Celsius or something. I would look at the stars. They would seem so close, all around me, as if I was floating among them. I would listen to the purr of the engines and the rush of the jet stream. The moon, if there was one, would be so bright.

You see, you don't have to go as far as the edge of the atmosphere and beyond. In these days of modern air travel anyone can be an astronaut. When you board any jet aircraft and soar towards the underside of the Heaviside layer you practically become a spaceman. You might not feel the effects of less gravity but you are certainly leaving the earth. Even if it is only temporary.

Not only this, by leaving the planet's surface for a long period and then returning to it, you are playing with time. You are juggling it. In principle if you keep winging in one direction around the planet you can make time stand still. Not only that, you can also travel back in time, or, conversely, zip into the future. It's a modern miracle. A kind of magic.

Furthermore, touching down can be a seriously alien experience. It's almost as if you take off on one planet and hours later land on another. Especially if you land somewhere completely foreign. Nobody speaks your language, they look different, they dress differently. Sometimes they are eating the weirdest stuff. The smells, the sights, the sounds can all lead to a sensory overload. Couple all that with the warping of time and, well, it's quite an eye-opener. That is, of course, if you can keep your eyes open. Long-distance air travel takes its toll.

Time itself can be manipulated. In the end it will return to normal if we so desire but it is not necessary. We can bend time. However, at some point we will lose it or gain more than we can use. We don't even have to leave the safety of solid ground to do it. Time even moves in one place. For some reason seasons have been given their own time. So, even standing still, time is fluid, moving this way and that around us.

There are costs associated with toying with time. They are not purely financial. If you skirt the globe and dodge the sun your body will experience it. You will suffer physically. Night will become day for your physical clock. You will spin out. You will lose all sense of place and time.

And you think witches talking to the dead is strange. The world of the living is far stranger.

BAMBINA

Naples International Airport was small and relatively deserted in comparison to Barcelona. To call it an international airport was stretching the truth. It consisted predominately of a collection of prefabricated sheds. The terminal was badly in need of an upgrade. This had its advantages. As there were very few services in the terminal, people didn't hang around for very long. Even the shade population was absent. It seemed nobody in their right mind had any reason to be there longer than necessary. Even the security personnel were running a skeleton crew. Those that were there were noticeably lethargic.

Nobody batted an eyelid at them. Both Immi and Marilyn blended in with their overstated attire even more than they had in Barcelona. They were not out of place in the company of other purveyors of Italian fashion. They even received a few jealous looks from a pair of middle-aged women coated in heavy make-up and sipping espressos at a coffee counter.

The advantages of travelling within the European Union were apparent. All the security checks had occurred at departure. Upon arrival they grabbed their bags and walked out of the terminal. After surviving the flight, Anaïs was relieved that some part of their journey ran smoothly. Only now they were at a loss as to where to go.

Anaïs marched out of the terminal. Deserted or not, being in the enclosed space made her uncomfortable. Her gut feeling was that as long as they kept moving they would be safe. But where should they move to? Sojourner had bundled them onto the plane to Naples but had not given them a final destination.

The arrival terminal's automatic doors slid shut behind Anaïs. She stood on the footpath and looked to her left and right. There was not a car in sight, only signs directing them to where they could get a taxi or shuttle bus. She had secretly hoped the magical Morris Minor might miraculously appear once again, as it had in France.

The librarian had followed Anaïs out of the terminal. She stopped beside her and surveyed the deserted parking lot.

'Great, now what?' exclaimed Immi.

Anaïs shrugged. She turned to face the librarian. There was a sour look on her face. Anaïs lost it. Exasperated, she berated the woman. 'Stuffed if I know! Why do you keep asking me what to do anyway? I have no idea!'

The librarian took a step away from the little witch, pretended to be insulted and folded her arms. 'Sheesh.

It was just a rhetorical question.' She rocked her head from side to side and jibed Anaïs. 'What's got you all uppity? Get a grip!'

Her face flushed, her ears burning, Anaïs fumed. She took a deep breath and mustered her outrage. She opened her mouth to let the librarian have it.

'Stop!' Nan yelled in Anaïs's head. *'Enough!'*

Instinctively, the witch clapped her hands over her ears. This caused them to burn even more. She spun and shot a look of irritation at the shade. She went to give Nan a mouthful but thought better of it. She held her tongue.

'Maybe we should all just calm down,' said the caretaker. *'And have a good think about our next move.'*

Anaïs regarded her for a moment. 'Ok, Nan,' she said.

The librarian nudged the little witch. 'What did she say?'

Although she found it difficult, Anaïs maintained her composure. 'Nan said we should cool it and have a think about what to do next.'

'Wise advice. Well, we're here to fix your book. Maybe we should look for a bookshop?'

'Bookshops don't fix books. At least I don't think so.'

'Ok, fine, perhaps you're right.' The librarian scratched her head. 'Maybe somewhere else? I don't know. A printer?'

'Maybe, but can you speak Italian?'

The librarian shook her head.

'I know a bit,' said Marilyn.

'Great! Then you can translate.' Anaïs grinned at the shade. 'What do you know?'

'*I know* ciao *and* prego *and* bella *and*—'

Anaïs rolled her eyes. 'Thanks, but I think we need a little more than tourist Italian.'

Before the shade could respond there was a loud, sharp beep of a car horn. They all turned to face the origin of the sound. Parked on the curb was the smallest car Anaïs had ever seen.

Marilyn shrieked in a high voice. *'Oh, how cute. A Bambina!'*

'Oh, how cute. A Bambina!' echoed the librarian in a similar voice, with a broad grin.

Anaïs looked from one woman to another. *Were they twins?* She turned her attention back to the car.

The Fiat 500 was painted the brightest tone of yellow—canary yellow to be specific. Due to its size and shape, it resembled the bird in some way. This comparison was further emphasised when both its doors swung open like wings. It was inviting them in.

The librarian bent forward and looked inside. 'I'm assuming this is meant for us?'

Anaïs examined it closely. It was going to be a squeeze to fit all of them in. After the flight she didn't think she could handle sitting in a shade sandwich any more. She had even borrowed the librarian's coat to insulate herself. Her body temperature was only now returning to normal.

'I think you're right,' she said.

'Do you think it's related to the Morris Minor?'

'Possibly, but how do we know who sent it? It could

be a trap.' Anaïs looked around. There were a few people unloading bags from a taxi further down the road. Other than that, their little group was alone. After her experience in Barcelona and the black car that had followed them through France, she had concerns.

She pulled out her promptuary. There was no change. Except she could have sworn the pulsing light in the star looked a little brighter. She pressed it but there was no response from the book. She dropped it back in her beret.

The librarian walked around to the driver's door. 'Let's just get in and see what happens.'

'You trust it? I thought you were glad to be rid of small cars?'

'I've decided it's much better to go with the flow.'

Anaïs raised an eyebrow. She turned to Nan. The shade shrugged. *'Maybe she's right. What else do we have?'*

'Nothing I guess,' said Anaïs and ran her eyes over the car. 'Fine, let's get in.'

The librarian tilted her seat forward and ushered the shades into the backseat. Marilyn had problems negotiating the small opening and hesitated.

'Please, just get in,' said Immi. 'I know it's probably not up to your usual standards.'

'At least I have standards,' she quipped. She turned her back to the car and stepped into the vehicle butt first. She pulled her legs and arms in after her. The librarian tilted the driver's seat back into position.

It was a lot warmer than it had been in Barcelona. Anaïs removed the librarian's coat, opened the passenger door and tossed the coat in the floor well. She stuffed her gloves and scarf into the pockets of her own coat. She opened her anorak and turned her face to the sun. It filtered through the clouds and had a pleasant warm edge. She stood for a moment and let it heat her body. She hoped the confined surrounds in the car would be just as warm and she would not suffer from shade freeze once again. She kept the anorak on just in case.

Anaïs tilted her seat forward to allow the caretaker to get in. Nan performed a similar trick to Marilyn. Anaïs smirked at her. She slid into her own seat and the librarian did the same. Immi searched the console around the steering wheel and found keys hanging in the ignition. She pulled her leg into the car. Immediately, both doors slammed shut and their locks engaged.

The librarian snapped her head around and looked at Anaïs in panic. 'Maybe we made a mistake?'

The witch's face flushed with the same concern. Then she recalled Marilyn's words in the plane about avoiding worry. They gave her confidence.

'If we have, it's too late now,' said the little witch and forced a wry smile.

THE SORRENTO PENINSULA

Surprisingly, the Fiat was a less erratic driver than the Morris Minor. Anaïs had expected that, with its Italian pedigree, there would be a bit of fire in its fuel tank. But no, the Fiat was a very careful driver. It crept through the streets, winding its way through tenement housing estates and industrial areas. It had an aversion to main roads and preferred to keep to the back blocks.

Occasionally Anaïs caught glimpses of the great crescent-shaped Bay of Naples between the houses. The calm waters of the Mediterranean glinted in the afternoon sunlight. The ever-constant bulk of Mount Vesuvius overshadowed them as they skirted around its base. Anaïs leaned forward in her seat and peered up at it through the windscreen. The mountain was huge. It seemed to be pressing down on them. It made the little car feel even smaller than it actually was.

The vehicle picked its way fastidiously through the last streets to the edge of the urban sprawl. Eventually it was forced to resort to using the only road available. A narrow highway hugged the coastline, carved into the side of the steep mountain range which bordered the bay. It was only on this road that the Bambina showed a hint of speed.

Anaïs felt safe in the car. Its motor had a comforting hum. The car negotiated its way carefully, cruising in a fluid motion through the serpentine curves of the road. It was so smooth. Anaïs sensed it was protecting its precious cargo. Whereas the Morris Minor had been fixated on speeding to its destination, the Fiat took its time. It was meticulous, precise and pedantic. There was no rush, only calm. She had no idea where they were heading but Anaïs trusted they would be brought to their destination in one piece.

Apart from the purr of its engine, the car was almost silent. There was no stereo blasting out of its dashboard. The vehicle didn't even possess a sound system. Everything about it was basic. Everything was functional.

Anaïs drew her eyes away from the road ahead. Watching it was lulling her to sleep. She took off her beret and searched for her promptuary. It was easy to find. For some reason the book felt warm. She pulled it out and held it between her hands. It was more than warm; it was fever hot, especially the star on its cover. She brushed it with a finger and felt it burn like a glowing ember, scalding her. She sucked her finger to soothe it. The light that slowly pulsed from the star was definitely much brighter than it had been. Anaïs sensed they had very little time.

She had no idea what would happen if the promptuary truly overheated. Was it possible the handbook could present a fire hazard or, even worse, explode? She closed her eyes and held it tightly to her chest, being careful to avoid touching the star. She willed it to keep going, to hold out a little longer.

She whispered to it like a small child. 'You can do it. Just hang on for me.'

The librarian glanced down at her. 'What did you say?'

'I don't think we have a lot of time. It's very hot.' She held the promptuary at arm's length.

The librarian reached across to touch the book. Before she could make contact a spark snapped at her fingertips. She yelped and retracted her hand.

'I'm not sure I want to be in the car with that thing.' She massaged her fingers. 'Can't we at least put it in the back with them?' She indicated the shades. 'They might cool it down.'

'I doubt it,' said Anaïs. 'I'll hang on to it. It's staying with me. If it goes, I go with it.' She slipped it back into her beret. 'Let's just hope we don't have far to go.'

The librarian nodded grimly. 'Yes, let's hope.' She crossed her fingers and held them up. 'I don't think this will help, but it's worth a try. It's the only magic I have.'

INSTRUCTION MANUALS

The problem with instruction manuals is that no one fully understands them. That is, until they have actually made whatever it is a manual instructs. An instruction manual is written from the point of view of someone who already knows the inner workings of a piece of equipment. This presents a problem.

The writer of the manual has usually built whatever it is in a particular way. Sometimes there is more than one path to an end result. Often the manual's author will decide to omit a few crucial steps. To them, some steps may seem unimportant or they decide it is common sense. If this sense is uncommon to the readers, they hit a snag.

The whole idea of a manual seems counterproductive. You might think: if you already know how something works, why would you need such a thing? Particularly if it is useful only after you have constructed a piece of equipment. Then you can sit back and say, 'Oh! That's what you meant.' Once you have this knowledge, an instruction manual is superfluous.

There are certain ubiquitous blocks with little bumps on them. Modern Lego sets are one of the few pieces of equipment with manuals that come close to doing an effective job. This is mainly due to their use of images— pictures help. You are walked through stages of adding this block to that block in simple steps. However, they are also not perfect. For a small child they are difficult to comprehend. And that is exactly who they are intended for. Generally, an adult is required to explain the method of communication. For anyone who is colourblind, they also present a major problem.

Anaïs was not exactly a small child, but without a guide or instruction manual she had to rely on instinct. Her lot was not easy. She would have to harness the inner workings of her tool alone. It was a case of learning on the job. Only through trial and error would she learn its full capabilities. This is not an ideal situation, although, in general, information gained through practical usage tends to stay embedded in the brain. Learning on the job is often far better than going to school.

Certainly a school is useful in teaching you the basics, but, regrettably, they will also teach the unnecessary. You will learn subjects and exercises which, later on, you will never implement. This is a waste of time. Honing your skills requires knowledge within a certain set of parameters. All the extra stuff will only create a diversion. It will confuse things. Having done a

P J WHITTLESEA

course or studied is no guarantee you will successfully make use of any of the information gleaned. It is like having the instruction manual but not knowing what the intention is.

For witches, experience is key. Practical knowledge is far superior to regimented schooling. As witches cannot gather together in one place, a school is also impractical. Most of what they learn relies on what they pick up along the way. Almost everything they learn is immediately put into practice. It is a risky method of education. Not everything is going to produce the desired result. A slow, gradual and sometimes frustrating learning curve, it requires hard work. There are no shortcuts in witchdom, just as there are none in life. We all have to dedicate time and energy to acquiring useful knowledge.

Promptuaries work on the assumption the user knows what they are doing. Only by giving the correct command will the promptuary oblige and fulfil the user's wishes. You will first have to use your acquired knowledge in order to work out what it is you wish to achieve. A promptuary instinctively knows what to offer, but only if you ask the right question. It takes some practice and helps to have a plan of attack. But using it correctly will give the best results.

There is an inbuilt safety mode to protect the innocent from inadvertently blowing things up, but it is not infallible. Certain functions will be triggered whether you like it or not. It is far better to make the right choice in the first place.

Correct use of a manual will eventually get you to

the final stage of whatever you are trying to piece together. However, as I noted earlier, a decision may be made along the way to omit a fundamental step or two. This usually occurs with instruction manuals when we think we know more than we actually do. Only once a task is completed will you become fully aware which steps are crucial to the whole process. In most cases, you cannot take one step without first completing the previous one. It is complicated and patience is required.

Fortunately, witches are blessed with a heightened sense of logic. However, they do need assistance. It is advantageous to allow your witch's handbook to be your guide. A promptuary will try to help its owner and magically nudge them towards the right course of action.

Although Anaïs was still learning, if she stuck at it, she would eventually harness the full power of her handbook. She had to be careful, though. If she rushed the job she could put herself in danger. If she circumvented the fail-safe she would fail to be safe. And nobody wants that. There is no going back from magical mishaps.

If we understand the whole warped logic of a manual and take time to decipher it properly, there should be no disasters. Even if you are not a witch, follow your manual carefully. Try to understand it by putting yourself in the shoes of its creator.

AMALFI

The sun barely penetrated to the foot of the narrow valley. The steep, almost perpendicular cliffs rose on either side and blocked out its full strength. The town was sandwiched in the rift. Daubed in thick white paint, the houses lined the hillsides, covering them completely.

Amalfi had been a fishing village and centre of industry for centuries. It showed. Time had seen layers of construction build up and fill the confines of the valley. From where she stood in the harbour, Anaïs looked up at the jumble of buildings that cascaded down the hillsides. They flowed into the base of the gully and towards her as if there had once been a landslide and the buildings had surged down the slopes and collected at the bottom. Bare rocky cliffs formed a rim above it all.

Behind her the waters of the Mediterranean crashed against the large stone blocks that ringed the harbour. The waves were enormous and pounded loudly against the stone barrier. Anaïs looked out at the open waters and the landless line of the distant horizon. It appeared as though nothing interrupted the sea in its northerly flow. Spray hung in the air and salty droplets showered her. She moved away from the water's edge and made her way through the nearest archway to the relative shelter of the town's tightly packed housing. Nan followed closely on her heels.

They began to negotiate their way through the tapering streets. It was hard going. To call them streets was to go too far. It was a labyrinth. A jumbled sequence of dim corridors and alleyways zigzagged their way between blocks of housing. It was a city planner's nightmare, clearly built before wheelchair access was considered a necessity. Steep ramps transformed into narrow staircases, which dived further into dark tunnels and back out again.

Anaïs sensed they were gradually climbing the hill even though the alleyways rose and fell. However, she had no idea where they were. In the tight confines it was impossible to get a sense of direction. Occasionally she could see through a gap in the houses. She then spotted the face of the opposing hillside with its own farrago of buildings.

The beret on her head became too hot. She took it off. The source of the heat was not just from her own exertion. The promptuary added to the temperature. Anaïs wiped sweat from her brow with the back of her hand.

She pulled the handbook out of the beret, taking care not to touch the star on the cover. She held the promptuary out in front of her and used it to guide their way. In the dark stone corridors the pulsing light of the star provided some form of illumination. Even in its disabled state it was useful.

Eventually, they picked their way out onto what appeared to be a main central road. Only then did they have the opportunity to ascertain their true position. Looking down towards the harbour, she could see they had climbed about halfway up the hill. Rows of shops lined the road, which snaked its way down the hill. In contrast to the narrow corridors the road was thick with tourists.

Anaïs whispered to Nan. 'Maybe we can do some shopping?'

'Maybe later,' said the caretaker. *'Let's see about your book first.'*

They both jumped when the librarian jammed her finger down on the Bambina's horn. The road was just wide enough to allow a car to pass. Somehow it had also carved a path through the throng of people.

Immi stuck her head out the window. 'I told you not to walk, but you never listen do you?'

Anaïs stuck out her tongue. 'No, not to you anyway.'

The librarian chose not to respond. She rolled her eyes and flicked her head, indicating they should get in the car. Anaïs considered her for a moment and then decided she had a point. The Bambina knew where to go. She didn't, even though she sensed they were close to their destination. The road wound its way up the hill and seemed to lead to a dead end. Anaïs dropped the promptuary back in her beret and stuffed the hat in her coat pocket. Putting it back on her head was no longer an option. Following Nan's lead, she got into the vehicle.

'This is very familiar,' said Marilyn from the back seat.

Anaïs half turned to look at her. 'You think you've been here before?'

The shade nodded. *'Yes, it's possible.'*

'I thought you could remember everything.'

Marilyn shook her head. *'Nobody remembers everything.'* She peered out her window and studied the shop fronts.

Anaïs swung around in her seat and turned her attention to the road ahead. The Bambina inched through the crowd. As they climbed higher, the road widened and the crowd dissipated. A few moments later the car stopped and cut its engine. Before them stood an ancient stone building. It seemed to grow out of the sheer cliff face it was nestled up against. Anaïs opened her door and stepped out of the car.

Heavy storm clouds hung on the hilltop at the pinnacle of the valley. Anaïs felt a tingle of electricity in the air. It raised the hair on her arms. As she walked the final steps up the road to the building the clouds receded in the distance, almost as if she was forcing them away with every step she took.

ANTICA CARTIERA

Except for its rear wall, the building was completely surrounded by water. Small streams were directed and redirected through pipes, tunnels and channels. Narrow aqueducts funnelled water into miniature waterwheels which in turn fed it back into the system. There was the constant sound of it gushing through the waterways, and the hiss of the spray as it tumbled down into large cisterns.

Anaïs had decided to go alone, leaving the others in the car. She picked her way between the channels, over small bridges and down a flight of stairs. She found the entrance to the building, a simple door with a decoration on the lintel above it. Into the lintel was carved an intricate relief of a book with open pages. The words *Antica Cartiera* were etched in the wood above it. In the centre of the door was a small imprint of a star, similar to the one on the front cover of her promptuary. Anaïs went to open the door but it beat her to it, swinging open in anticipation. She retracted her hand and hesitated. Nobody stood in the entrance.

Anaïs shrugged and stepped through the doorway. It was not the first time she had experienced objects moving of their own accord. Inside it was cold, dark, damp and clammy. She pulled her coat tight around her body and turned the collar up. She shivered. It felt like stepping into a room full of shades.

A single naked lightbulb flicked on and lit up the room. It was cave-like and bare. She heard footsteps descending a set of stairs at the far end of the room. They were carved out of solid rock and worn deeply in the middle by thousands of feet over the centuries. A man dressed in a body-length black tunic paused at the foot of the stairs. His face was obscured by a hood and she could only make out his lips.

'This way, Miss Blue,' he said in a deep voice. He turned and mounted the stairs.

'Thistle,' murmured Anaïs under her breath. She followed the man up the stairs. At the top they walked along a small corridor before descending down another set of stairs. All the while the sound of running water engulfed her on all sides. She had the impression they were moving under the sea. At the base of the stairs they passed through a doorway and entered another room.

It was full of ancient machinery. Everything was constructed of wood. There were pulleys and an enormous, slow-turning waterwheel. A gigantic press with a sizeable screw handle held a stack of paper over a metre high between its plates. The waterwheel powered conveyer belts which stretched at odd angles along the walls and across the room. From the shadows at the end of the room came a gentle, rhythmical pounding, like something heavy punching a pillow. Sheets of paper hung drying on horizontal poles suspended from the ceiling. A giant stone cistern stood in the centre of it all.

Anaïs stepped over a small ditch carved into the floor. A slow trickle of water ran out of the base of the cistern and along the ditch. The water flowed out through a small hole at the bottom of a nearby wall. The man stopped beside the cistern.

Anaïs furrowed her brow. 'Were you expecting me?'

The man spoke with a thick Italian accent but his English was impeccable. He measured every word. 'Certainly,' he said. 'We have just had a visitor. She advised us you were coming.'

'A visitor?'

'Yes. She did not say who she was but presented us with this.' He held out his hand. Draped over it was a thick piece of black cloth. Strands of gold thread ran through it, winking in the light.

Anaïs took the cloth from him. It felt strange. The material pushed back at her fingers. It was finely sewn, the thread spun by hand. A loose gold thread hung from the piece of cloth. Anaïs carefully pulled it out. The thread curled into a ball. Anaïs used her thumb to press it into the palm of her hand. It was spongy.

'I believe you have a book that needs repairing?'

'Yes,' said Anaïs, looking up from the ball in her hand.

'May I have it?'

Anaïs gave the cloth back to the man. She dropped

the ball of thread into one coat pocket and pulled her beret out of another. She reached into the hat and produced her promptuary. She considered the man for a moment, not sure if he could be trusted with her most prized possession. She handed it to him. The moment he took it she felt her body pulled towards the book. She felt herself drawn up onto the tips of her toes. She fought the urge to topple forwards and flexed her calves.

The man turned it over in his hands. They were covered in thick gloves. He ran his index finger around the edges of the star on its cover. He pressed the star with his thumb and held it in. Anaïs felt the pull on her body subside. She relaxed and stopped tensing her legs.

'Your promptuary has been damaged and will require a new index. We are making the pages at the moment but it will take some time.' He waved his hand towards the cistern. She looked over the edge. It was so tall her chin rested on the stone lip. The cistern was full of cloudy water. A large wooden pole stuck out of it. The man wrapped the promptuary in the black linen and placed it on a table. He moved back to the cistern and began to stir its contents with the pole.

'Shall I show you how we make your new pages?'

'Yes, please.' Anaïs nodded and grinned at him. He did not return the smile. Only the edges of his mouth twitched.

He picked up a flat sieve stitched into a square wooden frame and plunged it into the cloudy mixture. Carefully he drew the sieve out of the liquid and waited for it to drain. A thin layer of pulp coated it. He put the frame facedown across a semi-circular drum which had a layer of cloth draped over it. He removed the frame and the pulpy remnants were transferred to the cloth. It was the size of a small sheet of paper.

'Your pages are being made in another room. They require special treatment. I can be of no further service at the moment. We will have to wait. Your book will be ready tomorrow.'

Anaïs smiled and nodded.

'I would advise you not to go too far. Your promptuary will want to follow you, but in its present state I can keep it here with the cloth.' He nodded at the table. 'Your best option is to stay the night in the tavern across the road.'

Anaïs nodded. 'How will I know when it's ready?'

'We will find you.'

'I have one more question. What is the cloth?'

'I know very little about it. I am only a humble papermaker and do not supply the materials to make it. The woman who brought it here could tell you more.'

'But she's gone.'

'I'm sure you will see her again. She is one of your kind. If you need more answers you will have to consult your Organisation. We are mere artisans and our powers are of this world.'

'Can you at least describe her so that I know who I should be looking for?'

'She had a very pale face and the strangest eyes. I didn't dare look at her for too long. I sensed a power within her beyond anyone else who has been to these premises. She wore a wide-brimmed hat, a fedora I believe, and a long black coat with high boots. I can tell you no more.'

Anaïs sighed. The description was very familiar. Who was she? Anaïs was reminded of the woman who had played a part in Nan's death, the same woman who had been in Cornwall and perched on the basilica in Barcelona. Anaïs was certain she had also been the one attacking the Inquisitor at the airport. She made a mental note to ask Sojourner Pink about her next time they met. If there was a next time.

She offered her hand to the papermaker. 'Thank you for your help.'

He hesitated, unsure if it was safe to do so, and then took her hand and shook it. His hand was very cold and she shivered. 'There is no need to thank me. I am your humble servant, Miss Blue.'

'I don't believe in servants, sir. And please call me Anaïs.'

'As you wish. Anaïs it is.' The papermaker smiled for the first time. She caught a glimpse of his soft eyes beneath the hood. 'I hope you will be satisfied with the repairs to your book. If there is anything you need in the meantime you know where to come.'

'That is very kind of you. I will not forget your help.'

The papermaker put a hand on her shoulder. 'Come, let me show you to the door.' He directed her towards the stairs. Anaïs threw one last look at her promptuary wrapped in cloth on the table. She felt naked without it. She would take the papermaker's advice and not go too far.

As Anaïs went through the doorway and mounted

the stairs the book began vibrating. The room reverberated with the sound of its rumbling on the table. It lifted into the air but the cloth anchored it to the wooden surface. Only when Anaïs was completely out of the building did the promptuary stop struggling within its cloth prison. It settled back down onto the table, the only movement the light of the pulsing star on its cover, glowing through the cloth.

RAGS

I'm afraid that in order to fully understand what makes a promptuary tick, we will have to take a history lesson. I realise that for some people the idea of having to study anything at all is boring and tedious. Particularly if it is subject matter in which you have very little interest. I won't force you to read this, or warn that some archaic punishment will be dealt out if you don't. I'll leave that sort of thing up to Victorian schoolmasters. I think it's sufficient to say that without this knowledge, the loss will be yours.

So, let's learn about paper and book making in general.

At some point, in a very ancient civilisation, somebody decided it would be a good idea to write something down. Possibly because otherwise they would forget whatever it was they needed to remember. Chances are it was a shopping list.

I am not certain when we actually came up with written words and sentences, but even before they existed there were symbols. A single symbol could, and still does, communicate an incredible amount. We use them nowadays much more than ever, but it probably doesn't register how important they are. In fact, they are everywhere. If I suggest the image of a person shoving a stick into a mound of something resembling a pile of dirt, what springs to mind? Look out, workman working! Am I correct? It's a common symbol we see all over the place. If it was written out in full on a noticeboard we would probably not even bother looking. The simple shadow-puppet image is very effective. The bright yellow background also helps.

The symbol itself is of no great importance. It's more the fact it has to be written on something. In the case of the workman sign, it is cheaper and more efficient to write it down than pay somebody to stand around and warn people. Although it can be particularly irritating if they forget to take the sign away, in which case you prepare yourself unnecessarily for a danger that no longer exists.

Originally symbols were carved into things. Bits of wood, stone, even your spouse's leg. But if you wanted to write something longer you needed more room to do it. There is only so much you can fit on a leg. Also, it's handy if it's portable. A leg certainly fits the bill, but to stop it deteriorating it has to remain attached to its owner. Then you end up with the same problems associated with the workman sign. It's not efficient to drag around a notepad made of flesh and blood.

It took a while but mankind progressed to stone tablets, chalkboards, plant material, animal hide—ok, there is an alternative to keeping the leg alive. Finally, people took to writing on linen. Eventually the linen itself was used to make paper.

Many people believe paper is made from wood. It may be nowadays but for centuries it was not. It was made from used rags. Whole industries and people's livelihoods were dependent on the demand for the stuff. Such is the unusual preoccupation with things in the written form. You needed a lot of rags to make a single sheet of paper. And there are a lot of pages in a book. Someone had to collect the base material.

It was once considered an honourable, sought-after and useful occupation. Hence the words 'rag trade' I suppose. Although, I believe that now applies to the creators of fashionable clothing. They effectively provided the material necessary for traditionally making paper. I do wonder where all that used and pre-loved clothing ends up now. I, for one, would be quite chuffed with a piece of paper made from a Gucci ball gown.

Discarded garments, rags, tatters and other cellulose material is pounded and hammered to within an inch of its life. You really have to spare a thought for what a piece of clothing goes through. How insensitive are we? We should pause and have some sympathy for the victim. The torture doesn't stop there. The material is soaked and boiled until it dissolves in water. The resulting concoction is then passed through a sieve. The solid material that remains is dried. The end product is a reasonably flat, lumpy thing which we call paper. Leaves of this are then sewn together to form books.

Earlier I mentioned the whole idea of scrolls being

misinterpreted as magic wands. Scrolls were around long before books, but with the introduction of new, more compact formats, they swiftly went out of fashion. The portability of a manuscript or codex served to make it popular. I won't bore you with the details but I'm sure you can guess who came up with the idea for this new format. Witches got sick of lugging around rolled up reams of paper.

This brings us to the plight of the promptuary. A witch's handbook is no different to any other book. It goes through the same production methods. The pulping of rags, conversion to paper and sewing up into book form. What sets it apart is the material used to produce it.

The paper a promptuary is constructed from is derived from a very special form of linen. Not only is the linen special, the thread used to make it is also exceptional. This same thread is also used to sew the handbook's pages together. There are limited supplies of both these materials. Where they originate is a closely guarded secret. There are also very few factories which are capable of handling this precious material. Had the promptuary been in working order, it could have told Anaïs all these things.

Thankfully, she was not completely alone. The mysterious entity was not revealing itself but was certainly using all its connections to help her, facilitating things behind the scenes.

TRUMAN

Marilyn leaned forward in her seat. '*So, what happened?*'

'They're going to repair my promptuary,' said Anaïs.

'*And what are we going to do?*'

'We'll have to wait. I think it will be ready tomorrow.'

Anaïs sat down at the table. She had spotted the rest of her companions after walking out of the paper factory. They were seated around a table on a small terrace. It was in front of what Anaïs assumed was the tavern the papermaker had referred to. The librarian sipped on a coffee and looked at the witch over the lip of her cup. Nan sat next to her with her arms folded. She eyed the coffee with jealousy. Anaïs felt sorry for her. When she was alive, Nan had devoured coffee like there was no tomorrow. Anaïs had once pointed out to her that there was more of it running through her veins than blood.

Marilyn sat on the other side of the librarian in the last sliver of sunlight. She slouched in her chair and turned her face to the sun.

Anaïs snorted. 'What are you doing, trying to get a tan?'

'Of course, what's wrong with that?'

'You're a shade. I don't believe you can get a tan.'

Marilyn shrugged. *'It's worth a try.'*

'Forever the superstar,' said Anaïs sarcastically.

The shade pouted at her. Sitting next to Marilyn was a gnarled old man. He hung his head and stared blankly at his hands nestled in his lap. In the dark shadow of one of the smoke stacks of the factory that cut across the terrace, he was barely discernible. Anaïs immediately deduced he was another shade.

She indicated the man. 'Who's your friend?'

Marilyn cocked her head towards him. *'Oh, him? That's Truman. Truman Capote.'*

Anaïs was nonplussed. 'Never heard of him. Who is Truman Capote?'

The librarian put down her coffee cup with a clank and looked around. 'Truman Capote? What about Truman Capote?'

Anaïs pointed at the old man. *'This* is Truman Capote. Whoever that is.'

'Wow! Truman Capote,' said the librarian. She bent forward to get a better look at the shade. She sat back and shook her head at Anaïs. 'You know nothing, do you?'

Anaïs hunched her shoulders. 'What's to know?'

The librarian frowned at her. 'He was a writer, a really famous one.'

'Ok, if you say so. You should know. You're a librarian.'

'Well, sort of,' said Immi. 'I'd love to have a chat with him.'

'Not now,' said Anaïs and gave her a sour look. 'Could you give us a moment?'

The librarian flashed her eyes at the witch. 'Fine!' She sighed and picked up her cup of coffee.

Anaïs turned her attention to Marilyn. 'What's he doing here?'

'I don't know,' shrugged the shade. *'Why do any of us end up where we are? I suppose he likes it here.'* She moved her face slightly to keep it in the sunlight. *'I like it here.'*

'Does he know who he is?'

'I don't think so. I tried to communicate with him but got no response.'

'Do you usually get a response from other shades?'

'Nope.'

'Then how do you know it's this Truman guy?'

Marilyn pulled her compact out of her pocket. *'I used this.'*

'I didn't mean, how did you do it,' said Anaïs, slightly frustrated. 'I meant how do you know it's who you say it is.'

'I met him once, years ago. He was very nice to me. He was honest, genuine. Not many people were straight with me.'

'Where did you meet him?'

'At a funeral.'

'That figures,' said Anaïs. She rummaged in her beret and found what she was looking for. She slipped on her sunglasses. Under his camouflage the man looked practically the same. Apart from a small pair of spectacles balanced on the bridge of his nose and the fact he was slightly younger, he carried the same catatonic demeanour.

Anaïs waved a hand in front of his face. 'Sir, can you hear me?' He blinked but other than that he failed to react. He continued to stare trance-like at his hands.

'And?' enquired Marilyn.

'He's pretty far gone,' said Anaïs. 'I expect he's forgotten everything. I've met someone like him before. Not all shades are like you, Marilyn.'

'That's a shame. I guess I'm one of the lucky ones.'

'I guess you are. I have to admit I've never met anyone like you before, living or dead.'

The shade grinned and puffed up her chest. *'One of a kind?'*

Anaïs sighed. 'I wouldn't know about that, but yes, you are special.'

'Can we help him? I feel I owe him something. Very few people ever treated me with respect the way he did.'

'I kind of have my hands full,' said Anaïs. She looked across the table at Nan.

'Don't look at me, Anaïs. It's up to you,' said the caretaker. *'I do think you should help everyone you can, but I'm speaking from a dead point of view. Maybe you should wait until you have your promptuary back, though.'*

Anaïs yawned. 'Maybe you're right. I need a rest anyway.'

A waiter walked out of the tavern and up to their table. 'Miss Blue, your room is ready.'

Anaïs huffed and eyeballed him. 'Why does everyone call me that!'

NIGHTMARE

I t had to be a dream. It could not be real. How could it be? It was impossible otherwise. How did he get here? Why was he standing there right in front of her, in the middle of the street in Amalfi? Something was not right.

She tried to move but couldn't. She was frozen to the spot. She could move her body freely from the knees up, but somehow her feet were anchored to the ground. She looked down. Cobblestones encased her shoes. They had grown out of the ground and wrapped stone fingers around her. She tried desperately to shake the stone shackles loose. It was impossible. She strained against her shoes of solid rock. They didn't budge. She leaned forward and then backwards, almost losing her balance. It was pointless. There was nothing she could do. She was trapped.

She looked up. He was approaching her. The man in black with the shaved head. The Inquisitor. He was alone. Where was the dog? He always had the animal with him. That was good. That was fortunate. She would only have one foe to battle. She was certain without the hellhound he could be defeated. The animal was a force to be feared. He was just a man.

He measured his stride. He was in no hurry. There was no need. She could not run away. Frantically, she looked around for a weapon. There was nothing. She ran her hands over her body and down the heavy coat she was wearing. She searched for a bulge, a sign that there was something in its pockets. She felt nothing.

She grabbed her own skull and felt around the contours of her head. She ran her fingers through her hair. Her beret. It wasn't there. She never went anywhere without it. Why wasn't it there? The fan was in it. She could have used it as she had done before. She could have blasted him the hell out of there. Maybe even disintegrated the stone around her feet.

She shoved her hands in the side pockets of her jacket. She clawed with her fingers. The pockets were empty. Or perhaps not? There was something in the right one, something soft. She pried at it with the tips of her fingers. It was deep in the corner of the pocket between the folds. She pinched the edge with her fingernails and pulled out her hand. She held it in front of her face. It was a ball of lint. Or was it?

She placed it in the centre of her palm and closed her hands around it. She rubbed and rolled it between her palms. It grew, expanding and filling the void between her hands. A black substance oozed between her fingers. It looked like cloth. It coated the backs of her hands. It locked them together.

Damn! Her heart pounded. It encased her fingers like mittens and flowed to her wrists. It climbed her arms all the way to her shoulders. It continued to spread across them. In an instant it shot down her body. Dropping like a heavy curtain, it completely covered her torso and legs.

From her shoulders it slowly crept upwards. She felt warmth as it made contact with the bare skin on her neck. It wrapped so tightly she thought she would choke. It pressed against her Adam's apple. She stretched her neck to try to pull her head away from the stuff. There was no escape. It continued to spread.

He was centimetres away from her now, taking a last step towards her. He bent forward and nestled his head next to her own. The buttons on the breast of his coat were in her face. Then she lost sight.

The black moved up over her ears like the tentacles of an octopus. It covered her head. It ran over her forehead and down her face like a stream of warm water. She tried to blink it away but it was futile. She could not fight it.

The cloth forced her lids shut and continued its journey down over the rest of her face. It covered her mouth. She panicked and began gasping for air. *Calm yourself.* She could breathe a little. It was difficult but she managed. She wasn't suffocating. She felt cool air passing through her nostrils. The cloth was not airtight. It had left little holes under her nose. She inhaled deeply through them and out again.

She heard his voice. Close, so close, his hot breath in her ear. It echoed in her head.

'Got you!'

She grunted.

She screamed.

'No!'

With a rush of adrenaline, she threw her arms wide. Surprisingly, there was no resistance from the black coating. It shattered. There was a fierce rushing in her ears and a tinkling sound, like the crystals chiming on a chandelier blowing in the wind. She opened her eyes and immediately the sound stopped.

Strange. She was not standing. She was lying flat on her back. Something spongy was beneath her spine. Directly above her was a white surface. She peered at it closely, confused. The paint job had been heavy-handed. It was thick, glutinous and globular.

She was looking at a ceiling. A broad wooden beam supported it. The beam was stained black and cut a sharp, wide line across the centre of the white expanse above her. She turned her head to the right. She felt the softness of a pillow under her head. There was a window. Through it she could see a shape, the outline of the towers of the paper factory against a starlit sky. It *had* all been a dream. She was in bed.

She turned her head to the other side. Nan sat in an armchair, looking directly at her. *'Go back to sleep, Anaïs. Get some more rest. You have been dreaming.'*

Anaïs nodded and closed her eyes. She focussed on an image of Nan in her mind. She narrowed in on it. A still-shot of the smiling face of her caretaker. It blocked all other thoughts. The dream did not return and nor did the Inquisitor. She slept soundly until the sharp rays of morning sunlight hit her face.

Through the mist of sleep she heard the sound of knuckles rapping on wood. A door opened and then came the voice of the papermaker.

'Miss Blue? Your promptuary is ready.'

BATTLING EVIL

E vil has many faces. People generally become evil. They are not born that way. Certainly some are not aware they are perpetrating evil. Evil is a matter of opinion. Is there even such a thing as pure evil?

Is evil perhaps something that is only the result of a sequence of events? People do the strangest things, sometimes for no reason. Apart from spreading negativity, what is the purpose of being nasty anyway? Even if you are building an evil empire, you are constructing something. Even in evil there is growth.

Evil does not stand alone. It needs help. It has a group mentality. It needs support to be successful. Why would you practise evil if you have no one to share it with? Surely the evildoer is proud of their evil achievements.

Murder, arson, robbery. If you ran around doing these things and nobody batted an eyelid, would there even be a point to it? Evil requires encouragement. Evil requires an audience. It has to have a goal like everything else.

In some cases, the perpetrators of evil are unaware what they are doing is wrong. I am not excusing them, but it seems to me some will believe what they are doing to be for the greater good. So, is evil in fact just misplaced good? Is it all in the eye of the beholder? Or merely another viewpoint?

In the dark ages, also a loaded term, witches had to face evil. Perhaps more than at any other time in history. There were those out to get them. These scoundrels were no match for real witches. They chose to attack those who were defenceless. They chose to attack the innocent and the weak. Women and even children. Witches were not really the target. Their name was borrowed and then misconstrued.

In the Middle Ages the Witch-Finder General was one such person. He built a whole career around hunting down supposed purveyors of magic. Evildoers in his eyes. He gave them a name, labelling them witches, but only because he was lazy and probably a bit of a coward. Witches have a connection to something physical. At least in the minds of naturals. If he had said he was hunting down demons he may not have gained any kind of support. Not that he had real support. He forced his way into his dubious position. People need something physical to hang on to. There has to be a connection to reality. In general demons are rather difficult to see and it is difficult to prove they exist. Furthermore, if you go down that path you run the risk of raising something you can't control—the unknown.

He gave himself the job. He invented a non-existent position. I suppose in some way it could be seen as admirable. He was being an entrepreneur. He was out to make a living. He spotted a gap in the market and went for it. The fact that it was inherently evil and preyed on the weak was clearly not a concern for him. But it is always that way. The weak are easily duped, and not just the victims. Somebody also had to foot the bill for all the madness. The unscrupulous are also easily misled if they think they are getting a good deal. Naturals have a tendency to believe anything if fear is involved.

Whether the Inquisitor believe what he was doing was evil is debatable. He was certainly pretty good at generating fear. For him, this was relatively easy. Nobody really knew what his motivation was. The unknown was his greatest ally.

Clearly he had an obsession with getting the job done. Beyond that, he had set his sights on Anaïs. Or so it seemed. At the very least he was disturbing her sleep. For a witch in training this sort of distraction could be just as damaging. Even when he wasn't actually there.

If she was smart she should follow his lead. Not the evil part; more the work ethic. Just as he was doing, she needed to keep her focus on the job in hand.

REUNITED

It was where she had left it, lying in the centre of the table. The papermaker drew back the cloth covering it and revealed his handiwork. The promptuary looked brand new. The once tattered corners of its cover were neat and sharp. The pages were also no longer dog-eared. There were no smudges, scratches or stains on its cover. No signs of wear whatsoever. It looked like any other book that had just come off the shelf and never been touched. It was in practically the same state in which she had received it all those years ago. The cover sparkled. The star gleamed brightly, casting a warm glow on the ceiling above the table. It outshone the single lightbulb hanging in the dim room.

'You have a very special book here, Miss Blue,' said the papermaker.

'Anaïs,' she said and eyed him. 'What did you do to it?'

'Trade secret, I'm afraid, Anaïs,' he said, putting

emphasis on her name. 'What I have done is of no importance. I am just a facilitator, a humble artisan. I construct and repair. You had some damaged pages. I replaced them and the book did the rest. The magic is in the material, not in the making.'

Anaïs took his hand and shook it in gratitude. 'Thank you,' she said. 'May I?' She reached out to pick up the promptuary.

'Certainly. It is your book. My work is done. I must say your promptuary is the most extraordinary handbook I have ever worked on. Even in its debilitated state it continually made attempts to return to you. We did have quite a struggle but we found a way. I am pleased with the result and hope it functions normally.'

Anaïs twisted her lip. 'Honestly, I wouldn't know what normal is.'

The little witch slipped her hand under the book and cautiously picked it up. She handled it like an incredibly fragile object, a fine piece of porcelain. She balanced it on her flat, open palms. At first there was nothing, but then she felt a mild tingling in her fingertips.

The book sucked itself to her skin, creating its own vacuum and locking her palms to its cover. She felt its magnetic pull. A searing surge of power caused the veins on the backs of her hands to swell. The force snapped at her wrists and coursed rapidly up through her body. She stiffened and went rigid. A spike of adrenaline hit her and her heart began to race. It took her breath away. She felt a hot flush. The invisible force oozed from her pores like sweat and clothed her. She felt ensconced in it, almost as if coated in a layer of insulation.

Her entire body began to quiver. Her teeth chattered. She locked her jaw to stop them. She rocked on her heels. The papermaker cautiously took a step away from her. He eyed her with suspicion.

'Are you all right?' he whispered.

Her eyeballs were the only thing she could move. She rolled them round in their sockets to look at him. She had no idea what was happening yet strangely felt no fear. Her body was immobilised but there was a kind of tranquillity. She was one with her book. Reunited with a long lost friend. She wanted to tell the papermaker everything was fine, not to worry, but could not find the words nor even form syllables with her mouth. Her lips were numb as if under the effect of an anaesthetic. They trembled.

The star on the promptuary suddenly illuminated, flooding the room with blinding light. A wind emanated from the book. It blew the beret off her head. It felt as if someone had spat in her face. The blast shook the room. Centuries of dust, which had sat dormant on the rafters of the room, flew into the air. The whole room was covered in the stuff. The intense light from the star lit every speck and there seemed more than there actually was. It was like being in the middle of a snow storm.

The room was not the only thing affected by this second surge. A new, more intense explosion of power shot through Anaïs. She choked and spat out a mouthful of air. She gulped and quickly sucked fresh oxygen back through her teeth. It was stale and musty from the dank room. Particles of dust affixed themselves to her teeth. Some of them passed through and lodged in her throat. She choked and coughed. Her head began to swim. Panic set in. She moaned. It was too much. She wanted out. It was enough. She began to hyperventilate. She drew in several short, sharp breaths, desperately trying to get a hold of herself.

Nan's voice sounded in her head. She spoke softly. *'Anaïs, go with it. Don't fight it.'*

Anaïs tried to turn her head to look at her caretaker, but could not. She was still fixed in position. She clamped her eyelids shut and concentrated on the force flowing through her. She followed its path along her arms to its source, the book in her hands. The promptuary began to vibrate. The reverberations shot up her arms. The book threw wave after wave of pulsating power through her limbs. It turned them to jelly. She shook all over, her arms locked to the handbook. The shockwaves hit her as if she were gripping a jackhammer.

'Please stop,' she pleaded through her gritted teeth. A tear broke free of the corner of one eye and then a flood followed. They streamed down her face.

She screamed for all she was worth. 'Stop!'

The word echoed loudly off the walls, the ceiling and every other surface in the room. The power surge from the promptuary ebbed and suddenly stopped. The intense light was extinguished with it. She was released.

Anaïs expelled all the air from her lungs in one massive gasp. Her knees went on her. Falling forward she caught herself on the edge of the table with her hips. She folded at the waist and dropped the full weight of her upper body onto her elbows on the flat surface before her. She let her arms fall forward. Her wrists jarred on the table top. The promptuary bounced out of her hands and slid across the table.

The strain was too much for her neck, and her head followed her arms. She jarred her forehead on the hard wooden surface of the table. She yelped, let her head fall to one side and rested her cheek on the crook in her arm.

She arched her neck and looked at the promptuary. She stared at it for a moment. It lay there innocently— just a book. She screwed up her face and then turned her head to one side. She searched for Nan.

The shade was a few metres away, her arms wrapped tightly around a wooden pillar which supported the roof. There was a look of panic in her eyes. They flitted from Anaïs to the book and back again.

The little witch grinned at Nan. 'Well, that was an experience!'

Her whole body shuddered with a mixture of joy and relief. Anaïs began to giggle uncontrollably.

THE MESSAGE

Outside on the street, Marilyn hung over the witch's shoulder and admired the promptuary. Next to her, Truman stood with his chin on his chest, staring at the ground. He was very pale, even for a shade. His knees were slightly bent and it appeared as if he would sink down on them and collapse at any moment. Anaïs felt a pang of sorrow for him. Nan and the librarian stood near the entrance to the factory. The caretaker was sketching something in the sand at her feet. She seemed to be explaining to the librarian what had happened in the factory.

'It looks different, Anaïs,' said Marilyn.

'Yes, it does, doesn't it?'

'It must be a relief to have it back.'

Anaïs nodded and turned the book over in her hands. It felt good. The cover was warm and tactile. She felt one with it. It had become a part of her. Not the irritating object she had been lugging around in the past. Now it had power. Together they had power.

Intrinsically, they were linked. She rubbed the back cover with the palm of her hand. She pressed down on it. It was soft and malleable and moulded itself to her hand like a glove.

As she caressed the back cover, letters appeared. They swirled around the surface and assembled themselves in the centre. Two neat lines of text emblazoned themselves in gold lettering beneath her fingers. She retracted her hand. It left a vague imprint on the surface and then dematerialised. She read the words aloud, 'Memento mori.'

She scratched her head. *What did that mean?* She flipped the book over and ran her index finger around the contours of the star on the front cover. It sparkled where she touched it. A soft glow shone through the skin at the edges of her finger.

She splayed her hand across the cover. An unseen energy flowed through the centre of her palm. She watched with fascination as the veins on the back of her hand stood out on her skin. Purple lines drew their way up her forearms. She concentrated and held back its full force. If she focussed, she had control. She didn't dare relax for fear of repeating the experience in the paper factory. The energy the book emitted tensed the muscles in her triceps. It crept further, up through her neck. It entered her spinal cord and bored into her head. A flush of warmth coursed through her brain. She felt a wealth of knowledge flow into it. For a moment she felt slightly faint. She widened her eyes and flexed her eyebrows. It helped to clear her head. In her mind's eye she saw everything. She turned to the shade.

'Why don't you stop doing this?'

'What do you mean?' huffed Marilyn. *'Doing what?'* The shades eyes darted around.

'Being a cardboard cut-out of yourself,' replied Anaïs.

'What do you mean?'

'You spend the whole day obsessed with your appearance. You even try to disguise your disguise. I like you but not the fake you.'

Marilyn was insulted. *'It's not fake.'*

'Yes, it is,' said Anaïs. 'Why don't you just be yourself?'

'It's too hard. I prefer being this. To be frank I don't even remember who I was before. This is me now.'

'No, it's not.'

The shade would not be swayed. *'It is!'*

Anaïs considered her for a moment. Confronting Marilyn head-on would not work. She tried a different tact. 'Wouldn't you be happier being yourself?'

The shade shook her head. *'The thing is, people like what I have become. I wouldn't want to disappoint my fans.'*

'Marilyn, you're dead. Your fans won't be disappointed. They worship an image of you, a memory. Yours is perhaps the most famous image in the world. It's iconic and will never fade. It doesn't matter what you do now. Anyway, they can't see you any more. You can stop the charade. It's pointless.'

'Not to me!' The shade glowered at the little witch.

'Is that why you killed yourself? So you could stay this way forever.'

She eyeballed Anaïs. *'That's a bit harsh!'* The witch

folded her arms in defiance. Marilyn sighed. *'No, it had nothing to do with that. I was unhappy I guess.'*

'Why?'

'I wanted to be a mother.'

Anaïs raised an eyebrow. 'Oh, really?'

'Yes, I tried but it didn't work. There was something wrong with me—here.' She rubbed her stomach. *'I couldn't have kids.'*

Anaïs bit her bottom lip. 'I'm sorry.'

'Don't be. In the end I tried to accept it. It's not your fault. It's nobody's fault. I got used to it, sort of. Well, I tried to get used to it.'

'It's too late to do anything about that now, I suppose,' said Anaïs with a hint of sadness. 'But perhaps you could try to be yourself. You could stop acting.'

'I'm worried if I do that then there will be nothing left of me. I've been doing this for so long.'

'There's always something left of you. Just like the image of you people see on the outside, the part of you on the inside, the part you hide, can never die.' Anaïs paused. 'It is the *real* forever.'

The little witch continued, 'The image you worked so hard on will be forever implanted in people's minds. You don't have to sell it any more. I told you, you don't have to worry about that.' Anaïs reached out and clasped the shade's hands in her own. She fought the urge to shiver. 'Be yourself, Marilyn. Be the real you. Even if it's just for you. Your fans won't see it now. It's safe to come out. Stop being a shadow of yourself.'

Marilyn sighed. *'I have to think.'* She looked down at

the little witch and knotted her skilfully manicured eyebrows. *'Where do you get this stuff from?'*

Anaïs scratched her head. 'Beats me. Do you like it?'

The shade grinned and nodded.

'It's my job. I should try to be good at it,' said Anaïs. 'It's weird. The promptuary seems to be funnelling all this stuff. It's new.'

'How old are you anyway?'

'Eighteen.'

'Impressive. You don't look it.' The shade looked down her nose at the little witch.

'No. As you see, you're not the only one with a physical anomaly.'

'And you lecture me about my appearance?'

Anaïs flushed red.

'Sorry, being a teenager is hell. I remember. This must suck big time.'

Anaïs nodded. She took a deep breath and mustered her strength. 'Thanks, Marilyn, but we're not here for me. What do you think? Do you want to give it another go?'

'What?'

'Life,' said Anaïs.

The shade shrugged. *'I don't know.'*

'What makes you think you can't have a life like anyone else? What are you afraid of?'

'I don't think I can trust anyone. I got screwed around so much in the last one I don't want to risk it happening again.'

'It's a risk we all take. Nobody gets a choice in how it begins. But after that we do. It might not be easy, but we have to make the best of what we're given. Having a life is an honourable thing. You can do so much with one. Death is not going to get you anywhere. Wouldn't it be more fun getting the chance to see how a new one turns out? Wouldn't it be better to at least live a life on your terms instead of the one you just had. A life where you get to truly be yourself. Isn't that worth the risk?'

'I suppose so, but I'm scared.'

'Don't be. Fear is stupid. So are regrets.'

'That's a good one. Who said that?'

'You did.'

'Really?'

Anaïs nodded. 'Yeah, I read it somewhere. You also said you'd like to be delayed attending your own funeral.'

Marilyn laughed. *'Well, that didn't go according to plan, did it?'*

Anaïs smirked and shook her head. 'No not exactly.' She smiled at the shade. 'Look, even if it all turns to crap you can always come back and do it again.'

'Did I say that too?'

Anaïs shook her head again. 'I'm all out of quotes.'

'Pity, I seemed to have had some good ones.'

'Marilyn, the last time around you received the short end of the stick. Somehow you were duped. I'm sure the universe, or whatever it is, owes you a better existence. I don't control any of that stuff but it seems to me, you, more than anyone, should get the chance to have a happy and fulfilling life.'

Marilyn stared into space, lost in thought.

Anaïs moved into her line of sight. 'I don't know what I'm saying really. Am I blabbering?'

'A little bit, but it is good blabbering. Maybe you're right. Maybe I should give it another go.'

The star on the cover of the handbook began to blink and caught Anaïs's eye. She turned the book over and squinted as the piercing light flashed across her face. Anaïs heard the familiar wheeze of a large dog. It snorted. She looked up from her promptuary and down the street. He was back.

TAMING THE BEAST

The Inquisitor did not look happy. A snarl was frozen on his face. He lifted his hand, opened his palm and let the chain drop in the dirt at his feet. The beast looked up at him.

He growled at it. 'What are you waiting for?'

The animal snapped its head around and roared. It leapt from a standing start, bound into the air and careened down the street towards them. Anaïs's jaw dropped. The dog's paws pounded the surface of the road. Anaïs felt the thumping beneath her feet. She looked around frantically. Except for her and her companions the street was deserted.

She fumbled with her handbook. She was certain it could stop the beast. Only, she had no idea how to do that. She decided to point the star at the hound and hope for the best. She turned the book over and gripped it with both hands. She pressed her thumbs into the back cover and directed the star at the oncoming beast. She locked her shoulders and braced herself.

The animal hurtled at her. The hellhound spotted the book and veered from side to side, dodging her aim. She tried to follow its trajectory. A few paces before it reached her it suddenly made an abrupt turn. It flew past her, so close its fur brushed her leg. It had a new target. It headed directly for Nan and the librarian.

Anaïs let her arms fall, spun on her heel and went to follow the dog. She slipped and lost her footing. Her legs went out from under her and she landed full on her face. The fall knocked the book out of her hands. It took the wind out of her. She could taste blood.

She spat and cursed her body. During the fall and through the pain that followed she never took her eyes off the dog.

The animal locked it legs, splayed all fours and slid the last few metres towards the caretaker. In one fluid movement it crouched, bounded and hit her square in the chest. The nanny went flying. The librarian let out a high-pitched squeak, took a step back in panic and snapped the heel of a stiletto. She lost balance and landed heavily on her padded posterior.

The hellhound violently shook its great head and bared its teeth. A long trail of spittle flew from its mouth. The saliva slapped the ground sending a puff of dust into the air. The nanny sprawled on her back. She propped herself up on her elbows and scrambled away from the dog like a crab. The animal threw its head back and howled. The sound echoed off the steep sides of the valley. It paced towards the caretaker. Anaïs didn't need her sunglasses to see the fear on her face.

Before the dog reached Nan, two shadows obscured

Anaïs's view. They moved so fast she only saw a blur until they collided with the hellhound. It was Marilyn and Truman. The two shades slammed into the dog's flank and toppled it. The three bodies rolled as one across the street. A pall of dust, churned up by the knot of arms and legs, followed in their wake.

They came to a halt with Marilyn on the dog's chest and Truman strewn across its hind quarters. Marilyn jammed one hand down on the hound's throat and drove it into the ground. She whipped something out of her pocket with the other. She held it above her head— her compact. She flipped its lid open with her thumb and thrust the powder case's mirror in front of the dog's muzzle. Its red eyes flared.

The beast writhed under the weight of the shades. Incredibly they managed to temporarily pin it to the ground. Anaïs was struck dumb. She watched aghast as a bright red sphere of light grew in the space between the compact and the animal's eyes. It expanded rapidly. Licks of flame shot out from the glowing ball of illumination.

The sphere looked like pictures Anaïs had seen of the sun. There were black spots, and solar flares arced out from its circumference. She could feel the heat from where she lay on the ground. Marilyn turned her face away and arched her neck. The ball continued to grow. It completely engulfed both the hound's head and the shade's arm.

Marilyn coiled her legs and sprang backwards. She grabbed Truman by the collar as she leapt, dragging him with her. They crashed to the ground, the shade never taking her eye off the beast.

The fiery sphere continued to grow. It consumed the dog. There was a loud crackling sound like wood burning on a bonfire. The hound disintegrated. Flakes of ash rose in the air. A gust of wind swept down the street. It swirled around the cloud of ash and carried it away like a ball of tumbleweed. Within moments all that was left of the beast was a large dog-shaped scorch mark on the ground.

Anaïs wheeled around and searched for the Inquisitor. He was nowhere to be seen. The street was empty. She turned her attention back to the shades. They both lay panting on the ground. Marilyn sat up. Her entire right arm was blackened. A ring of light formed around it and made its way from her shoulder, down her limb to her fingertips. Anaïs watched with fascination as the seared flesh reconstructed itself. The ring disappeared and the arm returned to normal. The shade released her grip on the compact and dropped it on the ground before her. She flexed her fingers and pivoted her hand in front of her face. She scrutinised it for damage.

She turned to Anaïs and grinned, *'I told you I could deal with them, didn't I?'*

THE COMPACT

Anaïs stood over Nan and offered her a hand.
The caretaker grabbed it and pulled herself
up into a sitting position. The little witch
crouched down beside her.

Anaïs looked at her with concern. 'Are you ok?'.

'Yes, I'll be fine.' The shade brushed dust off her
elbows. *'Why did it go for me and no one else?'*

'I have no idea. At first I thought it was after me,'
said Anaïs. 'Maybe it didn't spot the other shades.'

*'Perhaps, but in the end it was certainly hell bent on getting
me.'*

'Yes, that is a worry. I don't want to lose you again.'
Anaïs gritted her teeth and eyed the shade with
determination. 'Nan, I won't lose you again.'

Another voice rang in the witch's head. It was not
the caretaker's.

'Maybe this will help.'

Anaïs looked up. Marilyn stood beside her. The

shade held out a fist and unfurled her fingers. In the centre of her palm was the compact.

'I can't take that, Marilyn. It's yours.'

'I insist. Please take it. You need it more than I do.'

Anaïs shook her head. 'No, you will need it.'

'Not where I'm going.'

'Going? What do you mean? Where are you going?'

'I've decided. You were right. The shell, this ...' She ran her hand down her body. *'This is not important. What's on the inside is. I want to try it again.'* There was a sense of purpose in the shade's eyes.

'Try what, Marilyn?'

'Life.'

'Oh,' Anaïs was taken aback. She stammered, 'That's great, really great. Are you sure?'

The corners of Marilyn's mouth turned up. She grinned and nodded.

'Only, I don't know how to help you,' said Anaïs. 'I can't snap my fingers and give you a new body. At least I don't think I can. I've seen it happen, but I don't know what I did or even if I had a hand in it. It just happened.'

'You have done enough, Anaïs. You opened my eyes.'

Anaïs sniffed. Her expression glum.

Marilyn knelt and took the witch in her arms. Almost immediately Anaïs's teeth began to chatter. She closed her eyes and stiffened. She gritted her teeth and reached into her coat pocket. The promptuary was there. She wrapped her fingers around it and the book responded. The promptuary turned to putty. It grew and oozed through the webbing of her fingers. It wrapped itself around her hand. A surge of energy raced up her arm. It flushed her entire body. In an instant the cold touch of the shade was no more.

Marilyn relaxed her hug and held the witch at arm's length. Anaïs opened her eyes.

'*Thank you,*' said the shade. She stood. Anaïs heard her take a breath. '*By the way, he's coming with me.*'

Marilyn reached out, wrapped an arm around Truman's shoulder and pulled him close. She escorted him to the centre of the road. A small car rounded the corner at the top of the street. It zipped down the road towards them. Marilyn lined herself up in the path of its trajectory. Before the car collided with the shades, Marilyn threw one last glance at Anaïs. She winked at her. Then the vehicle hit them.

Anaïs watched their bodies become transparent as the front bumper connected with them. The shades faded and dissolved as the car travelled through them until they were completely gone. She caught a momentary glimpse of the backseat of the car as it passed her. Two infants sat securely strapped into safety seats. Anaïs could just make out their heads through the window. One of them, a girl, turned to the witch and gave her the broadest smile. Anaïs smiled back. The car disappeared around a curve in the road further down the hill.

The little witch stared vacantly at the empty road. She fiddled with the book in her pocket. The promptuary had returned to its solid form. She ran her finger absentmindedly along its spine. Anaïs slipped her free hand into the other pocket of her coat. She dropped her shoulders. It had all been so fleeting. Why did they all have to go when she was just getting to know them?

There was something in her other pocket. She felt a square, cold, solid object. She pulled it out and looked at it sitting innocently in the palm of her hand. It was Marilyn's compact.

TEENAGE ANGST

Anaïs turned the compact over in her palm. Engraved on the back were two letter Ms. It reminded her of the words she had seen on the back of the promptuary. She pulled out her handbook and looked at the rear cover. The words were still there. *Memento mori.* What did they mean? Who could tell her? Sojourner Pink. Yes, she could tell her. If she saw her again. Where was she anyway? She said she would join them.

She sighed and dropped the compact into her pocket and hugged the book to her chest. It was good to have it back. She stared down at her shoes. They seemed so far away. She had really grown. She was still not used to it. The sudden change, the ageing. She frowned.

I don't want to grow up.

It dawned on her that there was nothing she could do about it. At some stage, it was going to happen again. Physically she was going to change. It was unstoppable.

Growth was going to occur whether she liked it or not. It depressed her.

She envied Marilyn. Shades were lucky in a way. They did not age. They stopped growing altogether. There was no more physical progression. They could look in the mirror every day, forever, and nothing altered. If they were fortunate they would die in good condition. It reminded her of what some long-dead rock star had said, or at least she thought it was a rock star. Live fast, die young and leave a good-looking corpse. Whoever it was had followed it to the letter. They were gone. As were so many more.

She knew that wouldn't be her destiny. Her life would not flash by. Her gut feeling was that she still had a long way to go. If things panned out anything remotely like Caput Mortuum's existence, she would be stuck in an earthly body for centuries. Barring situations beyond her control. If she could keep it all together. If she could stay safe and not fall victim to some terminal accident. Or succumb in a battle against forces more powerful than her own. She had no way to predict her future. No one did.

Witch or non-witch, natural or preternatural, the future was out of everybody's hands. No matter what you believed. There were just too many permutations. She didn't understand how so many people believed it was different. Thinking that everything was pre-ordained. That they could control their future. That it was written in the stars. You just had to deal with your lot, the one you created, and make sure you tied up all the loose ends.

What a bunch of fools!

Ok, it was unfair to think that way. She was no natural. She knew a great deal more about what made it all tick, the workings behind the scenes. She had the hidden information, the key to the universe. Sort of. There were mysteries, so much even she didn't know, but she was lucky. She should not gloat. Or blame people for what they didn't know. In most cases it was better they were kept in the dark. Some things should be kept secret. Knowing too much would break the system and bring it all crashing down around everybody's ears.

Even shades were not immune. The problems they had to solve were a result of how their lives had been led, not because they had started out with them. The problems had been created along the way, on the journey. That's what made it so difficult. If there was a grand plan or a book, perhaps something like a super-promptuary that mapped it all out, then it would be easy. There probably would not even be a need for witches.

She realised she preferred it this way. Thinking about these things actually made her feel better. It gave her purpose. Just having a purpose was important. She was lucky. She should enjoy what she was doing. She should not dwell in self-pity. She should be more positive. It was hard. But a challenge makes it all the more worthwhile. She decided she did not need to know it all. She accepted she had more time than the rest to expand her knowledge. That was exciting.

She looked across the road. The Bambina was there, and the librarian was helping Nan into the back seat.

Her Nan, her shade, her responsibility. After what had just happened she realised their roles had reversed. She had become the caretaker. Nan depended on her now.

The promptuary emitted a high-pitched beep. It repeated the sound over and over, steadily increasing in volume. *What now?* She flipped it open. The sound stopped. She stared at the page. A map materialised. A bright dot flashed in the centre. She grimaced. Was it trouble? Why did she have to be there? She sighed.

She shut the book and looked across the street. The librarian was behind the steering wheel, rapping her fingers on it. Anaïs sneered at her. Why was she always so impatient?

Fine! We'll go. Just give me a minute.

The thoughts that had been bothering her returned. Time stood still for no one. Change would come no matter what she did. It did not matter that she was a witch. She clenched the promptuary fiercely with both hands.

No, stop thinking about it. Forget about it. Just get on with it. Be positive. You can do this.

She cleared her head. A tenacious grin split her face and she challenged herself.

Bring it on!

Thank you for taking the time to read *Discovering Magic*.

All authors appreciate knowing what you think about their work. Posting a review and other feedback helps improve their writing, assists readers in discovering their work, and is generally accepted as good karma.

Please consider **posting an honest review** on the (web) store where you purchased this book, or on Goodreads.

Word of mouth is an author's best friend, and much appreciated.

Anaïs's adventures continue in

A New Source of Magic: Anaïs Blue Book Three.

The Mediterranean has never been more magical. Nor so dangerous. Pure evil rises from the depths.

From Pompeii to Malta, and the islands beyond, Anaïs Blue's extraordinary adventures continue. With her promptuary repaired, the little witch is now compelled to test its full capabilities.

It will be no holiday.

Her nemesis returns with supernatural help more powerful than even a witch can imagine. And to make matters worse, a war raging in the witch community threatens to upset the balance of the universe.

Anaïs is the universe's only hope. But is this a battle she can win?

Paperback ISBN: 9789492523242

ALSO BY P J WHITTLESEA

One man. No future. A rich heritage.

Indigenous urbanite Billy knows very little about his ancestry. He is quite content to let it stay that way. One late night out changes all that.

Stranded on a central Australian highway with only the stars and mosquitoes for company, he finds his future determined by a pair of unlikely saviours. And a mysterious supernatural entity.

In an effort to get home Billy embarks on a surreal odyssey. Not only into his heritage, but also into himself.

Read his remarkable story today.

ISBN: 9789492523006

ABOUT THE AUTHOR

P. J. Whittlesea is an author and singer-songwriter. Originally from Australia, he now resides in Amsterdam in The Netherlands.

To find out about new releases, promotions, special sneak peaks, and to follow his writer's journey, sign up to the author's **book club**.

Scan the QR code below for access.

As a special introduction you will receive a free digital copy of:
The City of Shades: Anaïs Blue Prequel.

Printed in Great Britain
by Amazon

30194137R00169